"You have beautiful eyes,
Trent murmured softly

"I would have sworn they were a golden brown...but now they're green." Deliberately he began removing the pins from her hair.

Carla swallowed convulsively. She couldn't move—couldn't even think. He was combing his fingers slowly through her hair, stroking her shoulder, her arm. He pulled her closer, and she could feel his warm breath tickling her skin....

Their lips met, and the spark that was always between them ignited. Excitement raced through Carla's veins as they caressed each other wantonly, caught in a web of mutual desire.

"Trent, please!" she finally gasped. "It's not good business...."

"We'll discuss business when I'm in your office," he growled against her neck. "Tonight I have something else in mind."

THE AUTHOR

Maris Soule knows the Midwest well—she lives in Michigan with her husband and two children on four and one-half acres of farmland. Chickens, pigs, dogs, cats— she says they raise everything, including a gardenful of vegetables every summer.

With her husband, Maris played the game "What if." What if a woman bank manager in a nearby town met a businessman.... The result was *No Room for Love*.

Books by Maris Soule

HARLEQUIN TEMPTATIONS
FIRST IMPRESSIONS
24—NO ROOM FOR LOVE

These books may be available at your local bookseller.

For a list of all titles currently available, send your name and address to:

Harlequin Reader Service
P.O. Box 52040, Phoenix, AZ 85072-2040
Canadian address: P.O. Box 2800, Postal Station A,
5170 Yonge St., Willowdale, Ont. M2N 5T5

No Room for Love

MARIS SOULE

Harlequin Books

TORONTO • NEW YORK • LONDON
AMSTERDAM • PARIS • SYDNEY • HAMBURG
STOCKHOLM • ATHENS • TOKYO • MILAN

Published August 1984

ISBN 0-373-25124-6

Printed in Canada

1

"WILL MR. PARKER BE BACK SOON?" a rich baritone voice asked from the doorway.

Carla looked up from the papers on her desk, pushed her reading glasses back on her nose and stared at the man who had entered her office.

His light brown hair had the casual perfection of a styled cut; his brown eyes were deep-set and alert. Lean and tall, he had an angular face: high cheekbones, chiseled nose and a strong jaw. Although he had broad shoulders, his navy pin-striped suit was a perfect fit and showed the signs of a tailor's touch. In toto he was a polished sophisticated businessman and for Roseville, Indiana, an unusual sight.

Undoubtedly he'd assumed she was one of the tellers using the manager's desk, thought Carla. Most people took it for granted a bank manager would be a man and she'd grown accustomed to the usual chauvinistic attitudes about women in banking. Still, it irked her.

"I'm C.J. Parker," Carla stated, rising to her full five feet ten inches. "What can I do for you?"

He stepped closer to her desk, his eyes moving slowly over her—from her knot of chestnut hair carefully twisted behind one ear, down the length of her slender figure to the hem of her charcoal-gray linen suit.

His bold perusal irritated her, and she raised her chin, her hazel eyes flickering with a trace of resentment. He would find nothing wrong with her appearance. She was careful to maintain a professional demeanor while on the job.

"Miss or Mrs. Parker?" he asked, his assessment complete.

"Miss Parker," she returned, certain he'd noticed she wore no wedding ring. But then, neither did he. She wished men also had a title that indicated their marital status. She dislike using Ms and felt men had a distinct advantage when they met her. Nevertheless, her smile now gave no hint of her inner thoughts. "And you're...?"

"Trent Campbell." He extended his hand and Carla reached across her desk for the customary handshake.

His grip was firm but not overpowering, his palm smooth. Quite a change from the rough and calloused farmers' hands that she touched daily. Obviously this man did not spend hours driving tractor or baling hay.

Carla motioned to a chair. "Won't you sit down, Mr. Campbell. What can I do for you?"

As he seated himself on the padded green chair across from her his eyes swept around the small office. The walls and curtains were a neutral beige, the carpeting a rich brown, and the furnishings limited to her metal desk, three chairs, and a set of filing cabinets. One wall displayed the bank's credentials and an oversized photograph of Thorton Wood, president of Indy State Bank and Trust. On a filing cabinet a large bouquet of zinnias added color to the otherwise austere room.

"I'm in Roseville on business and need some information," he began, then leaned back and shook his head. "I certainly never expected a woman banker here. Especially a young attractive woman."

"I am the senior officer of this bank," Carla coolly replied. "Believe it or not, women do rise above the position of teller nowadays."

Immediately he leaned forward, his tone apologetic. "I'm sorry. I didn't mean to imply a woman couldn't manage a bank. It's just that Roseville's such a typical midwestern farm community that I assumed the banker would be middle aged, rotund and—" he smiled "—male."

"Which disturbs you most? My age? My weight? Or—" her eyebrows rose behind her glasses "—that I'm a woman?"

"None of the above," he said quickly. "I assure you, Miss Parker, I'm not the least bit bothered to discover you're a woman. Merely surprised."

He nodded and sat back, leaving the fate of the battle in her hands. Realizing she didn't need to defend her position, Carla smiled a truce. "How can I help you Mr. Campbell?"

"I represent Campbell Industries," he explained, pulling out a business card and handing it to her.

Carla looked over his card and remembered reading about the company in the *Wall Street Journal*. Campbell Industries was a large corporation with diversified holdings. It was listed on the American Stock Exchange and based in Philadelphia. "You're a long way from home," she commented.

"My job involves a great deal of travel," he explained. "I suppose you could call me a trouble-shooter. If one of our subsidiary companies is having a problem, I'm the one called on to solve it."

"And what company brings you to Roseville, Mr. Campbell?" She couldn't think of any industry closer than Fort Wayne, and that was nearly thirty miles away. Farming was the commerce of this small Indiana community. And with a population of six hundred seventy-four, she knew practically everybody around Roseville—at least by sight.

"Actually I'm here because of a chemical plant we own in Chicago. Baker Laboratories has been doing amazingly well the last few years and has literally outgrown its present facilities. I'm looking for a new location for the plant...a site where we can easily expand. This week I picked up an option to buy a dairy farm in this area and I'm here to look over the land."

"The Clayton farm?" she asked, her eyes widening with surprise.

"That's the one. You know the place?"

"I know Henry Clayton, and I know his farm is up for sale, but I didn't know he'd sold it." In fact, Henry Clayton had been in the bank just that week, but the only topics they'd discussed were the weather and milk prices."

"Technically the farm hasn't been sold. Yesterday I signed a thirty-day option. Whether we buy or not depends on what I find during my visit."

"And what are you looking for?" Carla's interest was piqued.

He glanced at his watch. "Let me tell you over lunch. That is, if you don't have a previous engagement."

It was nearly noon and she was hungry. Carla looked down at the unfinished forms on her desk, her long dark lashes momentarily veiling her eyes. "I'm free for lunch. However, I do have to get these papers ready for the interbank pick up. If you don't mind waiting, it should only take a few minutes."

"No problem. In fact, I need to cash a check," Trent said, pulling out his checkbook. "Will you okay one for a couple of hundred?"

"I'm afraid I'll need more than your business card for identification." She smiled as he pulled out several credit cards and a driver's license. There was no doubt the man was who he claimed to be. Carla noted his picture didn't do him justice and that he was thirty-four years old and six feet two. She okayed the check. "One of the tellers will cash it. I'll be only a minute."

She watched him leave her office. Something about the self-assured way he moved fascinated her. It wasn't until he'd stepped into the lobby and out of view that her attention returned to the forms she'd been working on. Five minutes passed before she affixed her signature to the last page, slipped the papers into an envelope, and placed it on top of the pile of interoffice mail. A bank messenger would be by at one.

Her task finished, Carla removed her glasses and slid them into her purse. In the private bathroom off her office she applied a shade of red lipstick that gave her mouth a fuller more sensuous look, then pinned back a reddish-brown strand of hair that had slipped out of place.

It wasn't that she wanted to impress Campbell with her looks—she was realistic and knew she was no beauty—but she did pride herself on maintaining a neat, attractive appearance. And, she was willing to admit, she *was* looking forward to having lunch with Trent Campbell.

It had been nearly two weeks since she'd talked to anyone from outside of Roseville. As much as she liked the people around the town, most of whom were farmers or farmers' wives, she'd grown weary of listening to corn prices, complaints about the hog market, gardening hints and canning recipes. It would be interesting to have lunch with someone who lived in another part of the country and traveled a great deal.

She missed Fort Wayne. Carla knew it had been a good idea to move to Roseville, that by living in town and joining the local church she'd become a trusted member of the community. But basically she was a city girl. She liked the hustle and bustle of city life. Her only hope was that a management position would open up soon in one of the Fort Wayne offices.

Wood, the bank president, had to realize his mistake by now. She was certain he regretted his decision to name Dan Wright, and not her, manager of the downtown branch. Wood's comments at the last management meeting had indicated he was pleased with her progress and irritated by Dan's mistakes.

A frown creased her features as she thought about Dan, her ex-fiancé. She would never forgive him for the dirty tactics he'd used to obtain that appointment. The only positive aspect of the entire incident was that she'd discovered Dan was an underhanded, lying male chauvinist—and that she didn't really love him.

With a sigh Carla brushed a bit of lint from her

dark-gray skirt. Dan and the manager's position downtown were bygones. The present involved one Trent Campbell and what his presence in Roseville might mean to her branch. She didn't want to keep him waiting.

He was standing by the front door, his back to her, when she stepped out of her office. Carla paused a moment. Few men interested her, but she found herself once again carefully studying this one.

His hair had rich golden-brown highlights and was invitingly thick. He flexed his shoulders as if tired, and Carla could see the ripple of muscles beneath his suit jacket. She wondered what he would look like without a shirt, how it would feel to be held by those powerful arms.

Hey, get a hold of yourself! This is a business luncheon, not a date, she chastised herself. Then, with a smile, she entered the room. "Ready, Mr. Campbell?"

"Ready, Miss Parker," he nodded, turning to face her.

She informed the two tellers on duty of her plans. Trent held the door for her, and together they left the comfortable air-conditioned bank.

Outside it was hot and humid, July at its worst, and Carla felt beads of perspiration dampen her forehead as they walked along the tree-shaded sidewalk. Even her crisp linen suit felt limp by the end of the first block. "I pity the farmers who have to work in this heat," she said, searching for a topic of conversation.

"I don't know, I've always admired them. There's something honest about working the land. Besides, nowadays most of them have air-conditioned tractors."

Carla noticed he seemed unaffected by the temperature. As they strolled toward the town's only eating establishment Campbell was busily looking at the variety of small stores that lined Roseville's two-block business section. Nothing seemed to escape his attention.

"The town's not very big, is it?"

Carla had to laugh at the doubtful tone in his voice. "No, it isn't. But you won't find nicer people anywhere."

"What does one do for entertainment around here?" Trent glanced over at the two-pump gas station they were passing and at the three older men standing beside a rusted farm truck, talking and laughing.

"I asked myself the same question when I moved here," she confessed. "If you want to go out to dinner, or to a movie or a concert, you drive to Fort Wayne. It's half an hour away more or less, and a scenic drive. But most of the people around here enjoy getting together at each other's houses, going to the weekly bingo games, or attending an occasional VFW dance. One of those video-game arcades opened up last month, but it's mostly frequented by teenagers."

At the coffee shop Trent held the door for her, and they entered an air-conditioned atmosphere. The aroma of grilled hamburgers filled the small restaurant. Several farmers sat at the long counter, their denims stained and worn, while the local shop owners and employees, none wearing jackets or ties, congregated around Formica-topped tables. A few women, escaping the chores of home cooking or just taking time to be with their husbands, were scattered among the men. Carla and Trent, both in suits, stuck out like sore thumbs.

Although the restaurant was crowded there was an empty booth at the back of the room and Carla started for it, Trent close behind. She was halfway to her destination when a man at one of the tables pushed back his chair without looking and stood up, presenting an unexpected obstacle. Carla automatically stepped back—against a solid, forward-moving body.

She heard Trent's gasp of surprise, then felt iron-like fingers encircle her arms to balance himself as much as her. He held her close and Carla remembered wondering what it would feel like to be in his arms. And now it was happening.

His fingers were strong yet ever so gentle. His face was near hers, the scent of aftershave lingering on his cheek. It was a pleasant, very masculine smell. She could feel all of him against her, his sturdy legs supporting her additional weight. He was doing something to her senses she didn't understand, setting every nerve ending tingling with awareness.

Carla drew in her breath. This wasn't the way she normally reacted when a man touched her. He was making her feel soft and feminine, and totally helpless. Her mind was whirling. Trent was a stranger...a man she'd known less than an hour. What was wrong with her?

"You okay?" he asked, slowly releasing his grip.

"Yes...of course." Her reaction to him confused her. She'd bumped into him, he'd kept them both from falling, that was all. So why was her pulse racing, making her feel lightheaded, and her cheeks flushing?

"Sorry," mumbled the man who had caused the mishap. He was in a hurry to leave and barely noticed them as he pushed his way past.

But every other eye in the restaurant was now on the two of them. Carla knew about small-town gossip. Within an hour it would be public knowledge that she, the bank manager, had been seen having lunch with a good-looking man—a stranger.

Trent placed a hand on her shoulder and guided her past the table. She shrugged, hoping he might take the hint and remove his hand. She didn't like the feelings their physical contact was sparking, and she wanted some distance between them. But he ignored the gesture, keeping a hold on her until they reached the table.

Carla wondered if he could sense her tension. Years before she'd decided she would compete in a man's world as a man would. Her relationships with men when she was working were always conducted in a businesslike manner. She tried not to think of these men as being the opposite sex, for sex had no place in the day-to-day running of a bank.

Yet Trent Campbell—in some way she couldn't entirely understand—had breached that invisible barrier she'd erected and had swept her normally well-organized thoughts into a turmoil. When she looked at him she saw not the vice-president of Campbell Industries, but one very exciting man. And that was not good.

"You're very quiet," Trent said after they'd seated themselves. His brown eyes were searching her face. "I hope I didn't hurt you when I grabbed you."

"No, not at all. You have a very light touch." Carla remembered the feel of his hands on her arms—so strong, yet gentle—and the solid muscularity of his body. She knew she was overreacting to him and it bothered her. "I should have realized you were right behind me," she said. "I'm sorry."

"My pleasure," he said softly.

Carla stared at him, a frown puckering her brow. He could be flirting with her. But he was smiling, radiating a charm that added to his sex appeal, and she found it impossible not to respond. At last she also smiled, her hazel eyes becoming luminescent.

The waitress arrived, and Trent glanced over the menu, then ordered the chopped steak, french fries, dinner salad and coffee. Carla stuck to a chef's salad and milk. She'd never had a large appetite, and for that reason had always found it easy to keep her trim figure. Over the years her hips had rounded a bit, but the effect had merely softened some of her angles and added to her femininity.

"How did you end up in Roseville?" asked Trent, leaning back in the booth.

"The last manager had a heart attack and retired early. So I applied for the job."

"Am I the only one who thinks small-town banks are run by men, or did you run into some difficulties when you took over?"

Carla had to laugh as she remembered her first month in Roseville. "Wood—Thorton Wood, the bank president—warned me I would run into resistance, that the men around Roseville would be reluctant to trust a woman manager, but it still surprised me. For the first week the men around this town avoided my office like the plague. They'd go to Hazel—the head teller who's been here for years—before they'd come to me."

She shook her head and sighed. "Hazel was the first one I had to win over to my side. You would think one woman would be eager to help another, but she was of the old school. To her, women were tellers and men were bank officers."

"But you did win her over."

"When I realized that Hazel was doing my work, I invited her to dinner and we had a very frank and open discussion about the matter." A smile curved Carla's delicate lips and she looked at Trent. "Once I'd pointed out to Hazel that if she could do my job, so could I, she became my staunchest ally. After that when the men came to her she brought them into my office and gave me a glowing introduction. Not that I haven't run into a few diehards, but I guess that's to be expected."

The waitress served Trent his salad, and he picked up his fork. "I'm glad to hear the townspeople are willing to accept new ideas. That will make my job easier."

"Which brings us to the reason you're in Roseville," she reminded him.

"If the Clayton farm is suitable, we—Campbell Industries—will be moving Baker Labs to Roseville. Of course I'll have to check out the land, zoning, etcetera, etcetera, but I like the location. There's lots of room for expansion here and we wouldn't be far from a major city, railroad lines, or the Indiana turnpike."

The waitress brought his meal and Carla's salad, but Carla was too interested in what Trent was saying to eat. "Just how large is this chemical plant?" Henry Clayton, she knew, owned a good-sized chunk of land.

"At present Baker Labs employs a little over a thousand workers, but with the plans we have it should employ two thousand after the move."

Carla sat back in the booth. Two thousand workers. That meant two thousand families. Some would live in Fort Wayne, of course, but many would buy—well, they'd have to build them first—homes around Roseville. Oh, the changes that plant would make—the money it would bring into the community.... Carla could barely contain her excitement. Her brain was processing the information, projecting new accounts, investment capital and loans.

"How long before Baker Labs would move here?" she asked, still dazed by the possibility of managing a major banking office.

"I'll be in town two or three weeks. If everything checks out all right I'll sign the final papers with the Claytons and notify our architects. We should be ready to start construction within three months. With luck, a year from now we could move some of the operations here." He smiled, the lines around his eyes crinkling and giving his face a softer look. "I thought, as a banker you might be interested."

"I am." She leaned forward. "It's just what this town has needed. Young people don't stay in Roseville, not unless they have a family farm to take over. Sometimes not even then. Once they're old enough to leave home they go to Fort Wayne or Indianapolis, where they can find jobs."

"How do you think the townspeople will react to a chemical plant being so close?" asked Trent, cutting into his meat.

"It's hard to say." She had to be realistic. "Roseville is a typical Hoosier town—which means the people tend to be conservative, suspicious of strangers and fearful of new ideas. But lately the sagging economy has hit everybody. Plants have closed in Fort Wayne and unemployment is high. The possibility of local jobs would be very appealing."

"Is there a way I can talk to the business leaders as a group? Tell them my plans?"

"The Rotary Club meeting is Monday. I could call Bob Dolman, the president, and have him put you on the agenda."

"Would you? That would make my job easier." He buttered a roll and took a bite.

During lunch they continued to discuss the chemical plant, until Carla felt she had an accurate picture of Baker Labs, its research projects, inventory, sales and profits. Trent knew the ins and outs of the company, and she was amazed by his ability to remember so many facts and figures. His mind was quick, his insight keen. Qualities she admired in a man.

Not that she could completely ignore him physically. Call it chemistry or magnetism, she continued to feel an attraction, a desire to be touched by him. Her unusual reaction disturbed her and she asked him more and more questions about the company, forcing herself to concentrate on his answers and not think about the sensuous curve of his lips.

When they left the restaurant, Carla barely noticed the heat. Her thoughts were racing. She'd ask Jan, at the main office, to run a check on Campbell Industries and Baker Labs. Not that she didn't believe Trent, but Carla liked to do her own research. Her father had taught her that the more one knew about a client the easier it was to work with him. The lesson had paid off for her father in the insurance business, and was paying off for Carla in her career.

Before they reached the bank Trent stopped her. "I plan to spend the afternoon visiting the Clayton farm and finding a place to stay, but I'd like to take you to dinner tonight."

Carla hesitated. The idea was tempting, she hadn't been out to dinner in weeks. But there was the matter of her physical attraction to Trent. That disturbed her more than she liked to admit. "I'm sorry, but I make it a policy not to date customers," she finally responded, softening the refusal with a warm smile.

"Who said anything about a date?" he asked. "Early in my travels I discovered it's the banker who knows the community best. I need more information about the area and you're the bank manager. If you'd been the man I expected, I would have extended the same invitation. Are you telling me it's different with a woman?" His eyebrows rose and she had no doubt he was issuing a challenge.

"Of course not. I simply didn't understand your invitation," Carla brusquely responded.

"And if you'd been a man, Miss Parker," he continued, "I would have suggested you bring your wife or girlfriend along. I extend my invitation to include your fiancé or boyfriend."

"I have no fiancé or boyfriend," Carla informed him, before she realized how easily he'd extracted that personal information. With a smile, she faced him squarely. "And will you be bringing your wife or girlfriend?"

There was a look of admiration in his brown eyes

when he answered. "No, Miss Parker. I am neither married, engaged, nor attached to anyone. It'll be just you and me. When and where shall I pick you up?"

2

The doorbell rang, and Carla took one quick look in the mirror. Friday afternoons were always busy, and she'd barely had time to bathe and change since getting home from work. However, her tight schedule had also been a blessing. It had given her little time to think about spending an evening with a man whom she found sexually attractive.

Trent had said tonight wasn't a date, so she'd dressed accordingly. Her hair was freshly twisted into a knot at the nape of her neck, her makeup was subdued, and the dress she'd chosen was a versatile Qiana. Its surplice-front neckline, wide obi sash and figure-flattering skirt made it appropriate for an evening affair, while its stark ecru coloring and simplicity of line gave her the professional touch she desired.

She hurried down the stairs picked up her purse and opened the front door. Trent Campbell stood on her porch, wearing a midnight-blue vested suit, a white silk shirt and a striped tie. Carla wished she felt as cool and composed as he looked. The moment her eyes met Trent's her pulse quickened.

Pushing open the screen door, she put out her hand to shake his, only to discover he'd stepped to the side. Her fingertips touched his suit jacket; and electrical shock passed up her arm. She jerked her hand back in surprise, her carefully prepared speech forgotten, the simplest words suddenly difficult. "I'm... I'm ready."

"Then shall we go?" His smile was disarming and she was positive he could tell she was nervous.

She locked her front door. No one else in Roseville did, but Carla couldn't shake that habit. As they walked to his car she noticed that Miss Atherby, the librarian who lived across the street, was sitting on her porch watching them. Carla smiled at her, certain the old woman was making note of every detail of their departure. By morning half the town would know that Carla Parker had been out with "that stranger who's in town."

Trent held open the door of his beige Cadillac Seville and Carla slid into the passenger's seat. As he strolled around the front of the car he nodded a friendly greeting to Miss Atherby, whose eyes hadn't left them. In the few seconds Carla had to herself, she tried to calm her nervousness. Trent Campbell might be a good-looking man, but this was business... not a date. It was ridiculous to get so flustered simply because she'd touched his arm.

She'd learned a great deal about him that afternoon. Jan had returned her call within an hour, wondering why she'd asked about Campbell Industries... and specifically about Trent Campbell. Her report had been glowing. Campbell Industries was financially sound, had shown amazing growth in the last few years and had an excellent credit rating. Trent Campbell was the vice-president and second largest stockholder, his father being the largest. Together they held a controlling interest in the firm. Trent was regarded in the business community as being astute and diligent. He was also considered a prime catch by most of Philadelphia's women. Jan had added the last as her own personal comment.

"You look lovely tonight," Trent complimented Carla as he started the car, then drove down the quiet tree-lined street turning onto the two-lane country road that led out of town.

"Thank you, so do you...I mean...not lovely, but—oh, forget it!" She felt ridiculous. She glanced his way and caught him grinning at her.

"Want to try again?" he asked, the lines at the edges of his eyes crinkling in amusement.

"I think I'd better." She laughed. "You look very nice."

"Thank you."

There were a few minutes of awkward silence while Carla tried to think of something to say that wouldn't sound too personal or trite. Finally it was Trent who opened the conversation. "I'm staying at a hotel in Fort Wayne, but I'd rather be in Roseville so I could get to know the town better. Do you know of an apartment or house I could rent?"

"There are a couple of apartments above the hardware store, but I believe they're both occupied. You might contact Felix Gordon. He lives in the big green house just past the coffee shop and prints our local newspaper. He would know if there was anything available."

"Felix Gordon. I'll see him tomorrow," Trent nodded. "By the way, I went to the Clayton farm after I left you. It looks good. Of course I'll have to take some soil samples and get the drainage reports before I make a final decision. That, and have the zoning changed from agricultural to commercial."

"You enjoy your work, don't you?" Carla commented.

"I love it."

She could tell by his enthusiasm that Trent was looking forward to solving the problems of converting the dairy farm into a modern chemical plant.

"What about you? Do you like running a bank?"

"I hardly run the bank," she protested. "Thorton Wood makes all the major decisions. But I do enjoy managing the Roseville office."

Trent chuckled. "Henry Clayton said you're a darn...no...a damn good manager, even if you are a woman."

"That's certainly a change from six months ago," she laughed. Henry Clayton had been one of the men who had refused to ask her advice except for the simplest of banking matters.

"It takes some men a while to get used to seeing women out of the kitchen, but give them time." Trent pointed out the window to an apple orchard they were passing. "This is Johnny Appleseed territory, isn't it?"

"That's right." Carla was surprised that he knew about the man who had wandered across Indiana over a hundred and fifty years before planting appleseeds and preaching the "Good Word" to anyone who would listen. The legacy of Johnny Appleseed still lived on in some of the orchards they were passing. "How do you know about him?"

"He's legendary. I remember reading about him when I was a boy. I understand he's buried in Fort Wayne."

Carla nodded. "I like to think he was typical of the Hoosier spirit."

"Along with the Amish?" asked Trent, slowing the sleek Seville as he drew up behind a black buggy drawn by a horse and driven by a somber-looking bearded man dressed in black.

"Including the Amish," she agreed. Traffic coming from the opposite direction kept them moving at a snail's pace. "You'll discover they are one hazard when driving these country roads. Nevertheless, I enjoy seeing their horse-drawn buggies. The Amish remind me of another era, when life was simpler. There are several families of them living around Roseville, but they don't believe in banks, so I don't come into contact with them."

Trent glanced at his watch. "I made reservations for eight o'clock." Then, seeing a break in traffic, he eased the car around the buggy. "Actually, we should be there in plenty of time. I didn't expect you to be ready when I arrived."

"If I make an appointment, I believe in keeping it," she told him, but had to smile, remembering how frantically she'd rushed around in order to be on time.

"Then you're unique. I don't know why most women take so long to get dressed."

"If a man had to do his nails, apply makeup and fix his hair in a stylish hairdo, it would take him longer to get ready," she argued.

"A man has to shave."

"So does a woman. Can you imagine those pantyhose ads showing hairy legs?"

Trent chuckled, and she knew her allusion had amused him. "All right, I'll admit a woman does go through more fuss to dress up than a man, but I think a lot of it's unnecessary. If a woman would dress more ∧unctionally, she wouldn't have all that bother."

It was Carla's turn to laugh. "Shades of Henry Higgins, Mr. Campbell? Are you saying, 'Why can't a woman be more like a man?'"

"Well, no." He glanced her way, his velvety brown eyes skimming over her outfit. "But—"

"Look at yourself," she interrupted. "A three-piece suit is hardly functional in this heat, but you're wearing one and you certainly can't tell me that a tie is a necessity. The problem is, this is still a male-dominated society, so if a man considers something functional, it is—if not, it's deemed frivolous."

"And you'd like it the other way?" he asked, one dark eyebrow rising ever so slightly. "You'd prefer a female-dominated society?"

"Of course not. But I'd like to be judged as an equal. Take the business world, for example. If a good-looking man rises to a prominent position in a company, men say he's intelligent, capable and aggressive. Put an attractive female in that same position and everyone thinks she's sleeping with the boss."

"It's not always rumor," muttered Trent. "In my position I've met more than one woman who's offered me her body to get a promotion."

Carla glanced at him. She could see why. Damn, he was good-looking. The clean angles of his profile, the aggressive jut of his chin and his athletic build all added to his virile appeal. Going to bed with Trent Campbell would not be an unpleasant experience. Not, she quickly told herself, that she would ever consider such a thing.

"I'm sure you're right." She tried to get back to

the point, flustered by her thoughts. "But cases like that are far less frequent than cases where a woman's femininity works against her. Even the media plays down a woman's accomplishments. When Thorton Wood announced I'd been chosen to manage the Roseville branch, every reporter mentioned the color of my eyes, that I had a shapely figure and was unmarried. Not one of them mentioned my MBA or the training I'd had in credit investigation and lending."

"I hope they mentioned your beautiful legs," he said grinning.

"Mr. Campbell!" snapped Carla, feeling color rise to her cheeks. "That's exactly what I mean!"

"Trent."

"Trent what?" She stared at him in confusion.

"My name's Trent. If we're going to re-fight the battle of the sexes, I think we should at least be on a first-name basis. What do I call you? C.J. or Carla?"

"Carla." She shook her head in frustration. "I don't think you're taking me seriously."

"Oh, but I am." He slowed the car as he neared the outskirts of Fort Wayne. "You are an attractive, intelligent woman, obviously interested in banking, and struggling to advance in your career. How old are you, Carla?"

"Twenty-eight." She frowned. "What difference does that make?"

"None, really, other than you're lucky. Fifteen years ago few women had made it to your position. Now several major banking firms have female senior vice-presidents. You can't expect opinions to change overnight."

"Maybe not, but if women hadn't battled for their

rights we never would have made it to those top positions. On the average we're still not paid as well as men. Although," she added, "I personally can't complain about that."

Trent reached across the console and touched her hand. "All right, I'll agree with you. Keep fighting. But let's proclaim a truce tonight."

Carla looked down at the large, tanned hand resting on hers, then at Trent. He quickly glanced her way, smiled and gave her fingers a light squeeze. Then he returned his hand to the steering wheel. Was it a romantic gesture or merely a sign of understanding, she wondered.

"You're right. My battle isn't with you." It was refreshing to be with a man who didn't feel he had to put down a woman's accomplishments in the business world. "What do you think of Fort Wayne?"

"It's certainly not the sleepy little midwestern town I expected," he answered as they drove by a big industrial factory.

"Fort Wayne's the second largest city in Indiana." Even though her parents now lived in Indianapolis and she herself in Roseville, to her, Fort Wayne would always seem like home. Its streets and bridges were so familiar, its history was a part of her own heritage.

As they drove into the heart of the town, Carla told Trent how the Miami Indians, long before the white man arrived in America, had made the area their headquarters; how the French had set up a trading post—Miami town; and how the name was changed to Fort Miami when the English took command. She told him the story of the English using the local Indians to resist President Washington's armies and about "Mad" Anthony Wayne, who defeated Chief Little Turtle. "And that's how Fort Miami became Fort Wayne," she finished. "Today it's probably the most cosmopolitan city in Indiana."

"What impresses me is how clean it is," remarked Trent.

"Clean and progressive. There are many internationally known businesses located in and around Fort Wayne." She hoped her chamber of commerce spiel would help convince him that Fort Wayne, and specifically Roseville, was the area for Baker Labs. "Have you seen our main office?"

Twenty stories high, the main office of the Indy State Bank and Trust was located on Calhoun Street, its Indiana limestone facade facing the business district. From Thorton Wood's penthouse suite of offices there was a beautiful view of the junction of the Saint Mary and Saint Joseph Rivers, where they formed the Maumee River.

"I passed it this afternoon when I was looking for a place to stay."

"Would you like to meet Thorton Wood? If you're considering any large bank loans, I'm sure he'll have to be involved."

"When that time comes our accountants will take care of matters." He smiled her way. "I just do the running around, putting all the pieces together. And right now I'm perfectly satisfied to do business with the local bank manager."

Again she wondered if he was flirting with her or merely being friendly. Several things he'd said since picking her up could be taken either way. However, it would be safest to assume he was simply being friendly. If he'd had problems in the past with women throwing themselves at him, he certainly wouldn't be impressed by a small-town bank manager misinterpreting a few compliments.

When Trent turned his car into the hotel parking lot, Carla experienced a flash of déjà vú. How many times Dan and she had come to this same hotel, she couldn't recall. Their first date had been a drink in the lounge. Then there'd been dinners in the restaurant, dancing, and finally that one night when they took a room on the second floor—a celebration of their engagement.

She sighed as she remembered how happy she'd been. Dan had seemed so perfect. Discovering he could not accept her ambitious nature had been a terrible blow. But what had hurt most had been the realization that he was afraid of her. Frightened enough to demand she choose between her career and him, to beg her to withdraw her name from consideration, and eventually to lie to Wood about her.

"I said, are you ready?" repeated Trent, reaching across the console to touch her arm. The car was parked and he sat facing her. "You look miles away. Anything wrong?"

Carla snapped back to the present. "No, there's nothing wrong," she smiled. "Let's go."

They were quickly escorted to a table and given menus. A cocktail waitress took their drink orders, and in no time Carla had a vodka gimlet and Trent a martini. "To the future," he proposed.

Carla nodded, lifting her glass in a salute. Her future with this man would be limited. A few hours. Perhaps days. Then, in a couple of weeks, Trent would conclude his business and be gone. Pity, she thought, then sipped the tangy cocktail and sat back. "What was it you wanted to discuss tonight, Mr. Campbell?"

"Trent," he corrected, with that charming grin. "Carla, what I need is a thumbnail sketch of the community leaders. Nothing too personal. I'm not trying to pry into their lives, but since I'm proposing to build a chemical plant just outside of Roseville, I'd like to know how to approach each of them and what reactions to expect."

For the next hour Carla described Roseville's civic leaders—Dolman, Gordon, Swanson and Pierce—men whose families had lived in the area for generations, who owned large modern farms or in-town businesses. They controlled the township board and village council, were pillars of the community, and active members in the church.

The conversation was briefly interrupted when they ordered steaks and went to the salad bar, but Trent quickly picked up the topic as soon as they returned to their table. He asked incisive questions, delving into each man's character, and Carla found herself searching her memory for information that would not breach her banking clients' rights to privacy, yet would assist Trent. He didn't take notes, but she could tell he was absorbing everything she was saying, mentally filing it away for future reference.

Trent had ordered a bottle of Cabernet Sauvignon and Carla was amazed when he poured the last of the rich, full-bodied red wine into her glass. During dinner she hadn't been aware of how much she was drinking. She'd been so concerned with giving him the information he needed, she hadn't even truly savored the tender beef that was the restaurant's specialty. As the busboy removed their plates, Carla sat back.

She suddenly realized she was feeling lightheaded. No wonder it had been so easy to talk to Trent—the wine had loosened her tongue. She silently prayed she hadn't divulged too much information.

"Why did you decide to go into banking?" asked Trent, as the waitress offered her coffee.

Carla covered her cup with her hand and asked for a de-caffeinated brand before answering.

"It was the perfect choice for me," she explained, as the waitress filled Trent's cup. "Ever since I was little I've loved working with numbers. My father's an insurance salesman and I used to help him compile statistics and fill out forms. In high school I was a whiz in math, which became my major when I started college. But I soon discovered I was more business-oriented and switched to finance. After graduating, I tried working for a small private company, but there simply wasn't enough of a challenge, so I applied at several banks and was hired by Indy."

"How is it some man hasn't snatched you up by now?"

Carla stared at Trent, feeling a strange desire to reach across the table and touch his hand. It wasn't fair that one man should be so damned good-looking—and intelligent. His hair looked thick, his mouth inviting. Her fingers involuntarily twitched and she laughed self-consciously, embarrassed by her thoughts. "Mr. Campbell—Trent, let's be honest. I'm not the type of woman who sets many hearts throbbing. For one thing, I'm too tall. At five ten I'm either eye level with or looking down at half the male population. The other half are turned off by a career-minded Phi Beta Kappa. I frighten men."

"You don't frighten me."

For a moment Carla held her breath. Was it the wine that made his words sound so seductive, his eyes seem so velvety? She was relieved to see the waitress coming with her de-caffeinated coffee.

"Maybe that's because you don't know me very well," she answered, trying to clear her head. "If you did, you'd discover I'm very aggressive and competitive. I love a challenge. There are times I wish I could be like my younger sister, who's content to stay home and provide a loving atmosphere for her husband and baby. Then I realize that in a few months I'd be bored to tears."

"Not all wives are housewives. Some work," he argued.

"Sure, as long as her job doesn't interfere with her husband's career." Carla's tone was bitter, her eyes bright.

"Sounds like you're speaking from experience," he said softly.

Her gaze dropped to the cup of steaming black coffee on the table and she cradled it between her hands. When she had accepted Dan's proposal, she'd thought she'd at last met a man who appreciated her as she was. She'd assumed he knew she wanted to continue her career—but she'd been wrong. He thought she'd be satisfied to remain an assistant manager; that she would help *him* advance—be the "little woman" behind the man. What a shock it had been to Dan when she became his competition. For her, his reaction was proof enough that marriage and a career did not mix.

"I suppose am," she finally answered, then picked up her cup and swallowed a long draught of coffee.

To her relief, Trent didn't pursue the subject. They finished their coffee and he paid the bill. It was past nine when they started out of the restaurant.

Carla saw Dan first. He was holding the door for a petite brown-haired girl with a pasty complexion—Thorton Wood's daughter, Mary Anne. There was no way to avoid the couple.

Carla didn't realize she'd stopped until she felt Trent's arm casually slip around her waist, drawing her close to his side. She could sense his eyes on her, but she couldn't look away from Dan and Mary Anne.

"Well, well, well—imagine meeting you here." Dan's pale blue eyes darted from Carla to Trent. "I thought you'd forsaken Fort Wayne for the excitement of Roseville."

"Oh, even us country folk get into the big city once in a while," Carla managed. "How are you, Dan...Mary Anne?" She smiled as she greeted the young woman.

"We're just fine," Dan returned.

He looked dashing in his dark-blue blazer and gray slacks. Just under six feet, blond and so good-looking he could almost be considered pretty, Dan stole the hearts of most women he met. Carla knew. She'd been one of his victims. Then, remembering Trent, she made the necessary introductions.

"Campbell?" Dan repeated. "Are you from around here?"

"Philadelphia," Trent supplied, his manner formal and reserved.

"How in heaven's name did a man from Philadelphia end up in a town like Roseville? You did meet Carla in Roseville, didn't you?" Dan prodded.

There was a smile on Trent's face as he drew Carla even closer, implying a more intimate relationship than existed. "You could say it's a mixture of business and pleasure."

"What kind of business?"

Carla knew Dan would keep digging until he found out. He was like a terrier going after a bone, never giving up until he had the information he wanted, then using it to his advantage. Curiously she watched Trent.

"I'm looking at a dairy farm at the moment." Trent was purposefully giving the impression he was involved in farming.

"You don't look like a farmer."

"And just what does a farmer look like?"

Dan's blue eyes moved sharply over Trent's tailored suit and expensive leather shoes. "Certainly not so polished. The dairy business must be improving."

"It's a fluid market." Trent remained straight-faced and Dan completely missed the pun.

"Is it a very large farm?"

"Yes, quite large."

Carla wished Dan would drop the subject and let them continue on their way. She could tell he was impressed by Trent, and knowing Dan, that meant he would do all he could to gain Trent's approval.

"If you need anything while you're in town," Dan was saying, "just let me know. Carla and I are close friends."

She stiffened. How could he say such a thing?

Dan certainly should understand that the trickery he'd pulled with Thorton Wood had ended any claim to friendship. Trent casually moved his arm from her waist to her shoulders and began to toy with a strand of silky hair that had slipped from her twisted knot. Carla knew he was watching her and she tried to keep from showing her irritation at Dan.

"How's your father?" she asked Mary Anne, looking away from Dan.

"Oh, daddy's just fine," the young woman said. "You've certainly impressed him. Why, just the other night he mentioned you were doing better than he'd ever expected. Didn't he say that, Dan?"

Dan glowered at Mary Anne. "Your father also said the Roseville branch is a loser and should be closed."

"But it can't be, not when—" Carla started, then stopped when Trent's quick squeeze of her shoulders and shake of his head warned her to say nothing more.

"Why can't it be?" Dan immediately picked up, catching the exchange between Carla and Trent. "Is something happening in Roseville that I should know about?"

"No, nothing at all," Carla stated in all honesty. "It's just that Roseville is a growing community."

"Growing smaller," scoffed Dan. "That branch barely pays for itself."

"Honey, I'm getting hungry," Mary Anne gently complained.

"Sure, sure," he put her off. "I don't know what Carla's been telling you, Trent," Dan continued, his attention focused on the man opposite him, "but most of the owners of the large farms come to Fort Wayne to do their banking.''

"That isn't so," argued Carla.

Mary Anne tried again. "Dan, I haven't had a bite to eat since lunch."

Dan ignored her and gave Carla only a cursory glance before addressing himself once more to Trent. "We can offer twenty-four-hour banking, loans, mortgages."

"We do work for the same bank, if you'll recall," Carla bristled, barely able to control her anger.

"Dan—" Mary Anne tugged lightly at his arm trying to get his attention.

"Listen, we don't want to hold up your dinner." Trent smoothly directed his words to the younger woman, his warm smile changing her frown to a shy grin.

Dan glanced at Mary Anne, then back to Trent. "Perhaps you're right. Are you two going to the lounge? We could continue this conversation after Mary Anne and I have eaten. I'd like to tell you more about the services we offer."

Trent looked at Carla, noting her rigid posture and the strained line of her mouth. "Yes, I think an after-dinner drink is in order," he responded. "We'll look for you."

As Dan and Mary Anne moved on to the maitre d's station, Trent guided Carla toward the restaurant's exit. In the hotel lobby he paused only a moment, then started toward the cocktail lounge. Carla resisted, stepping back so he had to stop.

"Trent, please, if there's no further business you want to discuss, I'd like to leave now. I do have work tomorrow."

"No dice," he smiled, his arm tightening around her shoulders. "First of all, you look like you need a drink. Second, the night is still young. And third, I don't lie. I told your friend we were going to the lounge, so we're going."

"Dan is not my friend," grumbled Carla, discovering it was impossible to pull away from Trent's side without making a scene. Perhaps a drink would help. Running into Dan had upset her—that, and the news that Wood was thinking of closing the Roseville branch.

They entered a dimly lit bar with small tables closely spaced around a postage-stamp size dance floor. A combo was playing, making it difficult to hear or talk in a normal tone of voice. Trent pulled up a chair next to hers, his pant leg brushing against her skirt as he sat down. Carla looked at him, wondering why he'd insisted on coming to the lounge. She had thought Trent didn't want Dan to know his reasons for being in Roseville. Now it seemed he wanted to continue their conversation. Dan did have a way of making people believe he was exceedingly capable. Perhaps he'd changed Trent's mind about dealing with a branch manager.

"How about a brandy?" suggested Trent.

"Fine," she agreed, not really caring what she drank.

When they had their drinks, he lightly tapped the edge of his glass against hers. "Want to tell me about Dan?"

"What do you want to know about him?" She looked away from Trent, her eyes following the gyrations of the couples on the dance floor.

"It's obvious there's some animosity between you two."

"Animosity is the polite word." Carla looked back. "Listen, Trent, I don't really want to discuss Dan. Supposedly we're both professionals. Since I can't personally say anything nice about the man, I'd rather not say anything at all."

He chuckled. "I don't think Dan would be as considerate. What's he do?"

"He's manager of our downtown office." It galled her to say those words. The title should have been hers.

"Why was he so curious about me?"

Carla had to smile. "Dan thrives on knowing everything he can about everybody."

Trent sat back in his chair, slipping his arm behind her. For a moment he watched the dancers, a pensive look on his face, then he leaned closer, his mouth nearly touching her ear. "I don't want him to know about Baker Labs. At least not until I've presented my plans to the town's leaders. Have you told anyone?"

Carla shook her head and sipped her brandy. She was becoming more and more physically aware of Trent. His breath was warm and sent a tingle down her spine. His sleeve rested against the back of her dress, his hand brushing her arm, his fingers absently tapping the beat of the music against her skin.

"Good," he said, picking up his glass. "Not a word to anyone until after that Rotary Club meeting Monday. I'd just as soon get all of the facts on the table before rumors start flying."

"What about Henry Clayton? Won't he say something?"

Trent chuckled again. "When Clayton asked me why I was interested in his farm, I told him we were considering expanding an existing plant. Before I could go on, he started trying to talk me into farming the place. He never did ask what type of plant would be coming to Roseville. Let's dance."

Trent didn't give her a chance to refuse. Putting down his glass, he rose to his feet, took her hand and led her to the dance floor. Both tall, they made a striking couple.

In his arms, Carla relaxed, completely giving herself over to the music and the man. He guided her with the least effort, his graceful style of dancing carrying them easily over the small floor, turning them into a flowing unit. He pulled her closer and she rested her cheek against his and closed her eyes. The lead guitarist was singing, but Carla never heard the words. It was Trent Campbell who had captured her attention.

His face was smooth and the scent of his aftershave filled her nostrils. Her fingers moved slowly over his shoulder, feeling the taut muscles beneath the fabric of his jacket. Some time during the evening she'd forgotten this was a business dinner, not a date. As he made a slight dip, then a turn, the length of his body pressed against hers and she reacted as a woman, not a banker.

Her heart was racing, the blood coursing through her arteries until she felt warm and heady. Aroused by the intimate contact of their bodies, her nipples hardened, straining against the confines of her bra, their outline visible beneath the silky material of her dress. Her breathing was rapid, her cheeks flushed. The gentle pressure of his hips against hers made her stomach tighten and triggered off a wild set of thoughts.

What would it be like to make love with this man, she wondered. With Dan she'd tended to be passive. But somehow she couldn't imagine Trent being satisfied unless she also responded with equal intensity. There was a quality about him—a concern— she'd never felt with Dan. Intuitively Carla knew making love with Trent would be a totally new experience.

Then her common sense took over. Here was a man who had warned her earlier about women using sex as a ploy. She was reading far too much into a few casual gestures, turning a simple dance into a romantic encounter. It had to be the wine she'd consumed. The alcohol was affecting her logic. She had to stop thinking such erotic thoughts or she was going to do or say something very embarrassing.

"I think I'll visit the powder room," she told Trent as the music ended.

There she took several deep breaths, hoping oxygen would clear the haze from her head. She couldn't remember ever reacting to a man as she was to Trent. Something was wrong. She'd hardly known him a day, and already she was thinking of him as a bed partner. It just wasn't like her.

"Are you ready to go?" asked Trent, standing as she returned to the table.

"I thought you wanted to talk to Dan." The break hadn't helped. Trent still looked devastatingly handsome, his smile far too sensuous.

"I wanted an excuse to get away from the man."

He slid his arm around her waist. "I told him I'd look for him. I didn't say I'd wait." He paused at the exit and looked back toward the cocktail lounge. "I don't see him. Do you?"

"No—no, I don't," Carla laughed.

They were both still laughing as they walked across the parking lot.

3

TRENT PULLED UP in front of her house and shut off the motor. "Invite me in for a cup of coffee, Carla. I could use one before I drive back to Fort Wayne."

"I'm sorry," she apologized, turning to face him. "I should have met you at the restaurant. I never thought about your having to drive so far."

"No problem." He reached over and brushed the backs of his fingers over her cheek and smiled. "I've enjoyed being with you."

Before she could think of a response, he got out of the car. "All I have is de-caffeinated coffee," she told him as she unlocked her front door.

"Anything, as long as it's hot and strong." He looked around the narrow entry hall, with its flowered wallpaper, pale-yellow wainscoting and polished wooden floor. A stairway led up to the second floor, the banister shiny from a century of hands gliding over its surface.

"Why don't you go into the living room and relax, while I start the coffee," she suggested, closing the door behind them.

In the kitchen she quickly measured out the grounds, then poured water into the coffee maker. She was thankful to have a few moments to gather her thoughts. Although Trent had said tonight wasn't a date, his actions confused her. All evening he'd been attentive, caring and warm.

Under different circumstances she might have enjoyed a romantic encounter. He was attractive and certainly had a powerful effect on her. Ever since she'd first laid eyes on him, he'd fascinated her. But there was a matter of business savvy. Trent Campbell was a client—or at least a potential one—and she was the bank manager.

Her hand trembled as she plugged in the coffee pot. There was another reason she didn't want to get involved with Trent. Deep down she knew she'd be playing with fire. Her reactions when he'd held her had been far too emotional. She wasn't sure she wanted to find out what her response would be if he actually crossed that boundary and turned the evening into something more than a business date.

When Carla returned to the living room, Trent was standing in front of the massive brick fireplace, studying her collection of depression glass displayed along the white mantel. He'd removed his jacket and loosened his tie. His vest made a dark contrast against the white of his shirt.

She took a deep breath, then crossed the room to close the heavy, floor-length gold drapes that covered the two windows facing the street. The living room was spacious, with a high plaster ceiling and faded blue-and-gold striped wallpaper. Her Early American furniture—pieces she'd purchased at auctions and moving sales—blended perfectly with the house's late-nineteenth century architecture. Only the thick plush rug was new. She'd bought it soon after moving in. Its deep-blue color complemented the sofa and wallpaper, and covered several scratches and stains on the old oak floor.

"Your house?" asked Trent, turning to face her.

"No, I'm just renting. I didn't want to buy a house, then have to worry about getting rid of it when I moved. As soon as I can, I'd like to get back into Fort Wayne and a larger bank."

"Onward and upward." He smiled and walked toward her.

Carla couldn't draw her eyes away from his face. How quickly he'd analyzed her character. He treated her as an equal; yet in his presence she felt more feminine than she ever had. She wanted to impress him with her professionalism, but yearned for him to see her as a woman. The dichotomy of her reactions made her uneasy.

"Coffee on?" he asked softly, stopping directly in front of her.

Mesmerized, Carla nodded. His mouth looked sensuous in the dim light, his eyes captivating. Why did he keep staring at her?

"You know you're beautiful." He reached out and touched the side of her face. The contact of his flesh against hers sent a shiver down her spine.

"Trent?" She should turn away, explain to him that it was best for them to keep their relationship on a business level. She was the one who was always in control—as any of the men in her past would testify. But not tonight. Tonight she could barely mouth his name, her throat suddenly feeling very dry. She licked her lips and took another deep breath.

"You have beautiful eyes. This afternoon I would have sworn they were a golden brown... tonight they're almost green." His hand traveled to her hair and he began to remove the pins that held it in place.

"Trent, please..." she managed, not certain she wanted him to stop.

"Please what?" he murmured, as her chestnut mane fell to her shoulders and he combed his fingers through its silky mass.

Carla couldn't move. Her legs felt like lead. For once in her life, she couldn't seem to think straight. Her eyes drifted to his lips.

She was still watching those lips when he took her in his arms. Only as he bent his head toward hers did she offer one last protest. "We shouldn't—" she groaned, then slid her arms around his neck.

Carla wasn't sure what she expected. She'd been kissed by many men, but few had truly interested her. As Trent's mouth moved gently over hers, her lips responded with a will of their own. Forgotten was her usual reserve. She couldn't get enough of his kisses. He tasted so good, his tongue passing her teeth and coaxing her tongue into action.

The spark that had been present all evening suddenly flamed into a consuming fire and raced through her body. Her swift reaction alarmed her, and as his lips played along the edge of her mouth she gasped, "Slow down." Her legs were trembling as she realized her warning was to herself—not Trent.

"I've been wanting to kiss you all evening," he confessed, relaxing his hold, but keeping her close.

"I thought—" she stammered "—I thought tonight was strictly business."

"Not *strictly* business. I needed that information and what I said this afternoon about the bank manager being the best source was true, but the longer we talked, the more I knew I wanted to get to know you better."

Taking her hand, he led her to the couch. As he settled onto a firm cushion, he pulled her down beside him.

"It's not good business to...." She groped for the words, but could find none to describe her dilemma.

"When I'm in your office, we'll discuss business," he muttered near her face, feathering kisses over her cheek and down to her lips. "Tonight I have something else in mind."

His mouth covered hers before she could respond. Gone was the tender exploration of the previous moment, replaced by a hungry breath-stealing kiss. As his tongue forced her lips apart to penetrate the moist recesses of her mouth, he groaned. Slowly his hands moved over her arms, caressing her soft skin.

Carla tried to control her reactions, but it was a losing battle. Her mind was enveloped by a drugging euphoria. With one last effort, she moaned, "I shouldn't be doing this," then tilted her head back and allowed him access to her throat.

As the tip of his tongue danced lightly in and around her ear, he whispered, "Relax, Carla. Don't be afraid."

"I'm not afraid," she murmured, feeling his hands splay around her waist, his thumbs reaching up to touch the underside of her breasts.

Immediately Trent's mouth returned to hers. With an ease she could barely comprehend, he lifted and turned her, so that she was halfway across his lap, facing him. Before she could think about her new position, he loosened the front of her dress. One arm held her securely on his lap, while his other hand slipped beneath the smooth fabric of her bodice to touch the soft mounds of flesh contained by her bra. His palm flattened over one breast, gently measuring its fullness.

"Oh, Trent—" she breathed, shocked by the longing his caress was awakening.

He unfastened the front clasp of her bra and touched the velvety smooth skin. As he stroked each breast, her nipples hardened and began to ache. Closing her eyes, she let her head fall back, her hair draping over the edge of the couch, her breasts fully exposed to his view.

A groan of pleasure escaped her when he took one aching bud into his mouth and assuaged it with his tongue. Her lids fluttered open and she gazed at his light brown hair, then she closed her eyes again and simply let herself float along in a haze of sensual enjoyment.

Perhaps it was the effects of the wine she'd had at dinner, but she felt mellow and content. He kissed and licked her flesh, his hands moving slowly over her body. "Touch me," he prompted, and Carla reached up, her fingers shaking as she began to unbutton his vest.

When her fingers slid beneath the silk of his shirt, she felt him take in a breath. Quickly he removed his vest, tie and shirt, then slipped her dress and bra from her shoulders. Both of them were naked to the waist and he drew her close, kissing her as their chests touched and her breasts pressed against a mat of soft, wavy brown hair.

"Lady, you feel so good, I never want to let you go," he sighed, his hands moving across her back, as if he needed to know every inch of her.

"Trent, I—I don't know," she mumbled, certain she'd never felt more feminine than she did at this moment.

"Trust me," he whispered near her ear, then kissed her neck.

He lifted her from his lap and lay her back on the couch. Leaning over her, he bent his head and kissed her breasts. His tongue encircled each nipple and Carla pressed her blunt nails against his back as she tried to suppress a cry of ecstasy. Eyes closed, she was drifting on a cloud. Reality had turned to fantasy. Every nerve ending was sending messages of pleasure to her brain. Slowly he touched and aroused her.

She could feel his lips, warm and moist on her skin, traveling down over her taut belly. His hands moved to her knees, then back up, under her skirt, to her inner thighs. Her breathing quickened. What he was doing to her was more intoxicating than the wine she'd consumed earlier. She gripped his shoulders, arching her back.

"God, I want you," rasped Trent. "Let's go to your bedroom."

His words were like an alarm going off in her head as Carla suddenly realized the seriousness of his intentions. "Trent, no—please," she pleaded trying to sit up.

"Carla, don't fight what you feel."

Her skirt was twisted and her legs were exposed along with a bit of frilly white panties. He lowered his hips against her, pressing her back against the cushion, and Carla sucked in her breath. Through his trousers she could feel his arousal.

"No!" she gasped. "Trent...please."

He lifted himself slightly, looking down at her trembling chin. His eyes were filled with molten desire. "You want me. Don't deny it."

"No—yes." She bit her lower lip. What was the use in lying? Her body had already told him of her physical desire. How could she explain her reluctance? "I know this is the modern generation, when casual sex is the norm…but I haven't even known you twelve hours. You're going to be gone in two weeks or so. I'm the manager of a bank."

Panic was filling her. How had she, Carla Parker, the one who was always in control, allowed matters to get so completely out of control?

"I don't give a damn if you're president of the bank—you're still a woman!" he growled, trying to kiss her.

But she turned her face away and continued pushing against his chest with her hands. "I never meant to let things go this far."

Trent stared at her, his fingers gripping her arms. She was afraid to move. His thighs were pressed against hers and she knew he still wanted her.

Then, with a groan, he moved away and walked to the fireplace.

Carla hurried to dress, all the while watching his back. She could tell he was exercising a great deal of control. It was her fault they were in this situation, not his. She should have stopped him when he first kissed her, or at least when he began to undress her. But no, she'd let him go on, allowed him to believe she was as willing as he was. She'd behaved like a fool.

Slowly she saw the supple muscles of his shoulders relax. Then he took in a deep breath and turned to face her. Carla was seated on the couch, once more properly dressed, her skirt smoothed around her knees. Only her hair, tousled and falling wildly over her shoulders, served as a reminder of what had passed between them just minutes before.

"I'm not going to apologize for what I did," he stated, his eyes raking over her until she once again felt naked and vulnerable.

"I...I don't expect you to." She stumbled over the words, quickly standing as he approached the couch.

She was afraid he would try to kiss her again, but Trent made no move toward her. Instead he picked up his shirt and slipped it on.

"Think that coffee's ready?" he asked as he buttoned the front.

"I'm sure it is. I'll get it." She hurried out of the room as he loosened his trousers and began to tuck in his shirt.

By the time she'd returned with two mugs of coffee, Trent had put on his vest and was seated on the couch. He seemed relaxed and at ease, as if nothing had happened. Carla wished she could say the same about herself. Her hand trembled as she handed him his mug.

"Sit down, Carla," said Trent, as she stood in front of the coffee table, not quite certain what to do. "Here, next to me."

"I don't—"

"I'm not going to attack you."

She sat on the couch, keeping a safe distance between them. Trent didn't object, allowing her the space she needed.

"I said I wouldn't apologize," he began, "but perhaps I should. To you, I'm sure it seemed I was merely after your body. I want you to know that was not my intention."

"Trent, please. You don't have to say anything. It was my fault. I should have stopped you long before I did. I don't know what came over me." Embarrassed, she looked down at her coffee. She'd poured herself some, but her stomach felt tight and she knew she couldn't possibly drink any.

She jumped when Trent's fingers touched her arm. She'd been so absorbed in her own thoughts, she hadn't noticed when he moved closer. "I'd like to think you're as attracted to me as I am to you," he said softly.

For a second Carla stared at Trent, then shook her head. "I'm a practical woman. How I feel really doesn't matter. You're in Roseville on business, your stay will be short, then you'll be gone. I'm afraid I'm not willing to be a one-night stand—or even a two-week stint."

"Perhaps I'll take you with me when I go," he smiled.

"Slung over your shoulder like some prize?" Physically he could do it, she supposed, though she'd look ridiculous—all legs and arms. "I'm afraid I'm quite happy with my job and not breathlessly waiting for some man to carry me off."

"Oh, you'd go willingly." He leaned back against the sofa cradling his mug in his hand, his brown eyes twinkling.

"And what makes you think I'd want to go with you?" she challenged.

"Because I'm the man you need."

His smugness galled her and she rose to her feet.

"I've done perfectly well for myself so far, Mr. Campbell, and I'll continue doing quite well for myself after you're gone. Men want passive, servile, non-threatening women. Well, that's not for me."

"I'm not asking you to change. In fact, it's your drive I admire." Setting down his mug, he stood and walked over to her side. "Okay, maybe I rushed you tonight. I'm afraid that's a part of my nature. If I see something I like, I go for it."

"And if *it* doesn't go for you?" she asked, her chin raised in defiance at being compared to an object.

"Then I try to convince *it* that I'm an honorable man. Carla, I just want to get to know you better. Have lunch with me tomorrow. We can have a picnic, drive around...maybe go swimming. You could familiarize me with the area."

"I have to work," she responded, looking away as she realized how tempting his invitation sounded.

"Until noon. I saw your time schedule in the bank." He cupped his hand under her chin, turning her face back toward him. "I promise I won't do anything you don't want. Honestly, I'm not out to seduce you." His smile was disarming. "Consider this a business invitation...you'll be entertaining a client. Baker Labs will be one of your most important investors in years to come. Don't you think a little PR is in order?"

"I'm usually not finished until one," she said, knowing he'd touched on the one point she couldn't argue away. Public relations was a part of her job. Personal feelings aside, she couldn't chance annoying someone as important as Trent Campbell.

"I'll pick you up at one-thirty. You don't need to

do a thing but change into a swimsuit. I'll provide the car and food."

"No wonder your company sends you out to handle problems," sighed Carla, realizing she'd once again been manipulated into accepting a date. "I bet you could talk the stripes off a tiger."

"If I needed a tiger's stripes, I'd sure try," he chuckled, then leaned forward and gave her a quick kiss. "Now, if you don't mind, I think I'd better get back to Fort Wayne. I have a lot to do tomorrow before our luncheon date."

She watched him slip on his jacket and stuff his tie into his pocket, then she walked with him to the door. When he turned and wrapped his arms around her drawing her close, Carla tensed.

"Don't be afraid of me," he murmured, nuzzling her cheek. "I'm really rather a nice person, even if I say so myself."

"Humility isn't one of your attributes, I take it," she said, smiling. It did feel good to be held by him.

"'Fraid not." He kissed her on her forehead, then said good-night. As he strolled down the sidewalk toward his car, he was whistling, and Carla watched him until he drove away. After she closed the front door, she slumped against it.

Trent Campbell had broken down her defenses, taken her to the brink of passion. There was no way she could deny the feelings he'd aroused. She had lost control—and that frightened her.

"You're not ready," Trent stated, standing on the opposite side of the screen door.

It was obvious. Carla was still wearing the lightweight beige business suit and tan pumps she'd put on that morning. Trent, on the other hand, was casually dressed in a dark-red polo shirt, designer jeans and tennis shoes.

Bared, his arms were even more muscular than Carla remembered and were covered with pale brown hairs that matched the few exposed at the neck opening of his shirt. So much body hair struck her as exceedingly virile, and despite her determination to forget the night before, she couldn't. No more than she could stop the flutter of her pulse. A pair of expensive-looking dark glasses hid his eyes and she prayed he wasn't aware of the effect he was having on her.

"I'm not going with you," Carla began, thankful that her voice sounded steadier than she felt. "If you have any questions about Roseville or the Rotary Club, I'll be glad to discuss them with you Monday morning in my office. As it is, I have work to do this afternoon—personal work. I would have called you, but I didn't know which hotel you were staying at."

"Let me in, Carla." His tone was level and restrained.

"No," she stammered, losing her mask of control. "I've got too much to do.... I never should have agreed to go with you. I don't know what was wrong with me last night.... It must have been the wine."

Trent's eyebrows rose behind his glasses. "It wasn't the wine, Carla, and you know it."

Nervously her green-brown eyes flitted past him to the house across the street. Cora Atherby sat on a lawn chair in the shade of an enormous oak tree fanning herself with the morning newspaper and feigning disinterest. Nevertheless, Carla knew better. Miss Atherby might have gray hair, false teeth and arthritis, but she did not have a hearing problem. At sixty-eight, the former librarian missed little. If Trent made a scene—and the rigid line of his mouth gave Carla reason to believe he might—Miss Atherby was bound to tell everyone she met.

"All right, come in," Carla sighed.

As Trent entered the foyer she stepped back and looked up. It was unusual for her to have to look up at a man, and the sensation did nothing to ease her uncertainty.

"Now, what is all of this nonsense about work?" he asked coolly. "We made a date last night. Remember? Lunch, swimming and a little sightseeing."

"I shouldn't have. I wasn't thinking straight. I have clothes to wash...the house to clean."

Trent removed his dark glasses, his brown eyes quickly scanning the entryway, living room and kitchen. "Your house looks fine." There was an edge to his voice when his attention returned to her. "Why the excuses, Carla? Don't you trust me?"

Trust wasn't the problem—it was her own illogical reactions that bothered Carla. It seemed she had no willpower where Trent was concerned. Ever since he'd walked into the bank she'd been acting in ways that simply were not normal—and now was no exception. As she stared into his wide, expressive eyes, she felt herself giving in. "I trust you, but—"

"One afternoon certainly won't hurt. If it will ease your conscience, I'll even help you clean house when we get back."

That would be the day. She was almost willing to go, on that promise alone. "I'm sure a man in your position has better things to do than vacuum my rugs or dust my glassware," she returned.

"On the contrary. I've given myself the day off. In the back of my car is a picnic basket filled with delicious-smelling little boxes, and a bottle of Chablis, already chilled and packed in ice. Certainly a bank manager deserves a few hours of relaxation before she changes into a cleaning lady. You know what they say about all work and no play."

Trent smiled, the curve of his lips relaxing the firm line of his jaw and giving his face a beguiling charm. He *was* persuasive, she had to admit. The laughter lines near his eyes crinkled, and she wondered if he enjoyed life as fully as he seemed to. She wasn't aware she was staring at him—not until Trent reached out and lightly touched her cheek with the tips of his fingers. Softly he said, "Why don't you go change."

As she cooled off in a shower, Carla puzzled how Trent had so easily talked her into going with him. She'd spent a restless night after he left. Tossing and turning, she couldn't forget the feel of his lips on hers or the way she'd so readily succumbed to his caresses. Never before had she been so surely and deeply aroused by a man.

After hours of self-analysis, she had blamed her actions on too much wine and had vowed to watch her consumption in the future. But seeing Trent today, Carla knew her behavior had nothing to do with alcohol. Trent Campbell had an appeal she couldn't resist, stirring yearnings she hadn't even known she possessed—and that bothered her. She would have to watch herself this afternoon.

Toweling herself dry, then looking at her choice of bathing suits, Carla chose a conservative green and white maillot. Stylishly designed, the bathing suit complemented her bustline, yet minimized the curve of her hips. Not too sexy, she decided, and not too prudish.

Over the maillot she wore a red off-the-shoulder peasant blouse and white chinos. Tennis shoes covered her feet and only her thick chestnut hair, twisted into a soft knot behind her ear, remained as a vestige of the business woman.

"Ready?" she asked, draping a multicolored beach towel over her shoulder and coming down the stairs.

"Very nice," Trent murmured, his eyes quickly scanning her outfit. "You have a swimming suit?"

"I'm wearing it." Picking up her purse and dark glasses, she stepped to the door. "After you?"

On the way to Trent's car, Carla waved to Miss Atherby and smiled. She could almost hear the old lady now, telling her friends, "He was there again, that handsome stranger. That's two days in a row he's taken her out."

Deep down Carla felt a mischievous sense of triumph. Having her name linked with Trent's was really quite flattering.

As they drove out of Roseville and into the countryside, a cooling breeze from the air conditioner brought relief from the afternoon heat and Carla leaned back against the plush seat. Trent was right. An afternoon of relaxation would be a pleasant change from her usual routine. She would enjoy herself, but she would stay on guard for her own preservation.

"I tried calling Bob Dolman, the president of the Rotary Club, this morning, but he wasn't home," she informed Trent, feeling more comfortable discussing business, rather than sitting in silence or engaging in idle small talk.

"I know, I tried to get a hold of him myself. Think you'll still have time to set me up for Monday's meeting?"

"I'll see him at church tomorrow. I'll talk to him then."

Trent nodded. "If we move Baker Labs to Roseville our executives will be looking for new homes. I'd like to know where to direct them. Give me a picture of the housing patterns around here."

Carla laughed, pushed her dark glasses back up on her nose and looked out the car window at verdant fields of corn and soybeans. Only here and there did a farmhouse break up the gently rolling landscape. "Direct them to Fort Wayne. There are very few really nice homes around Roseville and certainly no pattern to the housing. A new ranch-style might be built next to a run-down centennial farmhouse.

There are a few newer homes just outside of town near the school, but not what a company executive would want to buy."

"Is there much of a turnover? Many places up for sale?"

"There's always a turnover. Farmers, like Henry Clayton, who get too old to work the land and have no one to take over—they have to sell. So do young people, who come here to escape the problems of the city, then discover country living also has its drawbacks and change their minds. The newer homes sell fast. The older ones usually need a lot of repair."

"In other words, if our employees want to live close to work, they'll have to build." Trent turned off the two-lane blacktop onto a gravel side road.

Carla agreed. "That or commute. There are some beautiful homes north of Fort Wayne."

Trent's eyes were darting left and right as he studied the farms they were passing. A combine cut through a field of red-gold wheat, spewing out straw to dry in the sun, while lifting life-giving grain into a truck that followed its progress. "I think most of our workers will like this area. Clean air...lots of room. It would certainly be a contrast to Chicago."

And Baker Labs would be a contrast to Roseville's small locally owned businesses, Carla mused. But it had to be. Dan was right: Roseville was dying. Without new industry, business would dwindle down to the necessities—a gas station, grocery store and post office—no more. Certainly no bank. For that reason alone Carla wanted Trent to like the area.

He glanced up to watch a turkey buzzard make slow gliding circles over a newly mowed field of alfalfa, then as if reading her mind, stated, "An increase in population would certainly improve your bank's financial position."

"Definitely." There was no sense in denying the obvious, especially after Dan's comments the night before.

"I would say, offhand, that you and I can mutually benefit each other." Trent reached across the console to lay his hand over hers.

A mutually beneficial relationship. She stared down at the long fingers covering hers, at his blunt well-manicured nails. Well, that was the way of business. You scratch my back, I'll scratch yours. And as long as he didn't ask anything dishonest of her, there wasn't anything wrong with helping him. In the long run her own career would benefit. Still, she couldn't help wondering who interested him more—Carla, the person, or C.J. Parker, the bank manager.

"You know, Trent, you don't have to wine and dine me for my cooperation," she said. "I'm well aware of how much Baker Labs will benefit the bank and my position."

"The wining and dining have nothing to do with business. I asked you out purely for the pleasure of your company." The car hit a rut and he grabbed the steering wheel with both hands. "Damn. As nice as a ride in the country may be, these roads leave something to be desired."

As the Cadillac bounced along, its shocks getting a thorough workout, Trent asked more questions about the area. Trying to paint an honest picture, Carla described the plight of the farmers around Roseville. Without exaggeration she told him about the men and women who struggled to eke out a living, all the while fighting rising costs, unpredictable weather and fluctuating market prices.

"If they stay small they can't compete," she explained, "but if they over-expand they get too far in debt and one or two bad years can put them under. Today's farmer has to be an economist, agronomist and wizard...all rolled into one."

"Sounds like you admire them."

Carla pondered his remark. When she'd first moved to Roseville she'd looked down at the unsophisticated, philistine men who walked into her office. Now she knew them personally, appreciated their provincial ways and was aware of the long hours of hard work they put forth each day. "I guess I do," she admitted. "What they may lack in polish, they make up for in generosity."

"Turning into a country girl?" Trent asked, one eyebrow rising ever so slightly above the rim of his dark glasses.

"Never," Carla assured him. "Careers don't go far in the country. If Baker Labs comes to Roseville and the town grows, then fine, I'll stay here. But otherwise I want back in the city just as soon as possible."

"I forgot, onward and upward."

"Anything wrong with my wanting to better my position?" she demanded coolly.

"None at all, as long as you have your priorities straight."

"Such as?"

"When to place humanity ahead of career. I've seen too many goal-oriented men—and women— who think nothing of stepping on or destroying others to gain another rung up that ladder of success. Believe me, it isn't worth it."

Wasn't it? Dan had stepped on her and now he sat in a plush downtown office. "Good guys don't always come in first," she retorted.

"But they sleep better at night."

"I sleep fine."

"Good." He smiled, stopping at a corner to wait for a tractor and grain wagon to pass. "We're almost there."

"There?" Carla eyed him curiously. She'd been under the impression they were aimlessly driving around the countryside—now it seemed Trent had a specific destination in mind.

"I stopped at the gas station in Roseville before coming by to pick you up. The man there—the owner, I think—gave me directions to what he called a nice little lake."

"Neil Higgins? Redhead with glasses?"

"That's the man." Trent nodded, then grinned. "What a talker. For a minute I was sorry I'd asked if he knew of a good place to go swimming. I didn't think I'd ever get away. Especially when he heard it was you I was taking."

"Oh no," Carla groaned. Next to Miss Atherby, Neil Higgins was the biggest talker in town. Now there would be no denying the rumors. "What did Neil say?"

Trent's grin widened. He steered the Cadillac off the gravel road, onto a one-lane drive that skirted a corn field, and headed toward a large wooded area. "He said, for you he knew just the spot. I gathered you did him a favor?"

"I approved a loan on some shaky collateral," Carla explained. "That's the advantage of a small town. I know Neil's good for the money."

"Well, he said you're one in a million. Told me to mind my manners." Trent imitated the gas station owner's midwestern drawl.

Carla smiled and looked out the window. They were slowly approaching the trees, the car bumping over mounds of dirt and dipping into depressions. "Are you sure you know where you're going?"

As if in answer to her question, Trent steered the car to the left. Before them stretched a long narrow lake. Its presence was concealed from the main road by the trees, but the tire tracks leading directly to the water's edge were proof that many others knew of its existence. An empty car and boat trailer were parked under the shade of a maple tree.

"Good enough for a picnic?" asked Trent, pulling the Cadillac up beside a Chevy. "Your friend said it's a private lake, but we're welcome to use it this afternoon. He also said some of the best bluegill and perch in the country come out of these waters."

At the far end of the lake, bobbing beneath the shade of a large willow tree, a rowboat could be seen. A single figure sat hunched over in the boat, fishing pole in hand. "Think we'll disturb him?" Carla asked as they got out of the car.

"I doubt it. He's too far away and we'll be long gone before he's through fishing. You take the blanket, I'll get the food." Trent reached into the trunk for a large red picnic basket.

Within minutes they had a blue blanket spread out over the grass. As Trent began to unpack the basket, Carla realized how late it was and how hungry she'd become. Her stomach growled as Trent expertly popped the cork from the bottle of Chablis then reached for one of the two g-stemmed glasses in the picnic basket.

"I really shouldn't," Carla pleaded when he offered her the filled glass. She remembered too clearly what had happened the last time she'd had alcohol.

"How can we have a gourmet feast without wine?"

Carla relented, then leaned back and sipped the dry vintage as she watched Trent open plastic-coated cardboard boxes and place before her marinated cherry tomatoes, crusty white bread, Rock Cornish game hens, fresh strawberries and green grapes. It was a meal fit for a king—or a queen.

"How.... Where did you get all of this food!" she exclaimed.

"The hotel. D'you know they have a master chef? Great fellow, Pierre. He even let me help." Trent popped one of the tomatoes into his mouth then sighed in satisfaction as he licked his fingers clean. "I fixed these myself."

"I'll bet." She took one, the small red fruit bursting in her mouth, its acidic flavor blending with the herb marinade.

For a while, eating—savoring the hint of rosemary on the chicken, the shallots in the butter and the basil on the tomatoes—occupied both of them and they said little. But as their appetites were satisfied, talk came naturally. The food and wine relaxed Carla and soon she forgot her qualms about coming, and merely enjoyed being in the company of an attentive articulate man.

"Absolutely perfect," she sighed, when her plate was clean and her hunger sated. Flies buzzed around the near-empty cardboard containers, and Carla automatically closed each of them. "My compliments to the chef and to you for turning a picnic into an epicurean delight."

"I'll tell Pierre you liked it," Trent said, refilling his wineglass before leaning back on one elbow and gazing up at the blue sky. "I needed this. It seems nice to have a day to relax. Lately I've been constantly on the go."

"You're on the road a great deal?"

"Quite a bit...or flying from company to company. And when I'm not, I'm kept busy at the home office. My father will be sixty-six next year. He'd like to retire." Trent sipped his wine, then reached over to seductively run a fingertip along the contour of her arm.

Goose bumps rose on Carla's skin. Electrifying, tingling sensations raced down her spine as his finger moved lightly up her arm. This would never do. She couldn't let him know how sensuous she found his touch. Quickly she asked, "Do you have any other brothers or sisters in the business?"

"I have only one sister. She's a lawyer, happily married and the mother of two children. Campbell Industries doesn't interest her."

"How is it you've never married?" Carla heard herself asking. The question, she knew, had been hovering on the edge of her mind since the night before.

"I was married once, many many years ago, but it just didn't work out. It's hard to say whether to lay the blame on our youth, the fact that I was away from home so much on business trips, or on Rita's constant demands for attention, but we decided a divorce was the only solution. She remarried, has four kids and we're good friends. I've even played golf with her husband."

"You didn't have any children?"

"No, thank goodness. Not that I didn't want some, but considering how the marriage turned out, it was for the best. Even when it's uncontested, a divorce is never painless."

There was a sadness to his words. Not knowing what to say, Carla raised her wineglass to her lips, then seeing it was empty, put it down.

"Last night you told me you've never been married," said Trent, sitting up to pour her the last of the Chablis. "But I'm sure there have been some men in your life."

"A few."

"Anyone really serious?"

"Just one." *One miserable mistake.* Absently she bit her lower lip and gazed down at the light amber liquid in her glass.

Trent noticed her sad expression. "It didn't end very long ago, did it?"

Carla sighed. "Eight months ago."

"Want to talk about it?" Trent asked, moving closer to her side.

"No." She shivered as his hand touched the sensitive nape of her neck.

"Sometimes it helps to talk," he said, pulling a hairpin from her severe hairdo. "I know."

She'd never told anyone the truth, not even her parents. She certainly wasn't going to tell a man she barely knew. "Trent, shouldn't we clean up this mess?" Leaning forward and away from his touch, she brushed crumbs from the blanket.

"Leave it," he murmured, reaching out and snatching another bobby pin. "It was Dan, wasn't it?"

"How did you know?" she gasped, stopping her clean-up to stare at him.

"You told me last night." Deftly he began to remove the remaining pins from her hair.

"I said nothing of the sort." Suddenly realizing what he was doing, Carla jerked her head back and tried to stop him. But it was too late. Unfettered, her long chestnut tresses tumbled to her shoulders.

Trent studied the softening effect the more casual style had on her face and smiled. "Body language sometimes tells more than words. You were too tense around him—too upset. Do you still love him?"

"Love Dan?" Her eyes sparked green. "I wouldn't love him if he was the last man on earth."

Trent considered that, then shook his head. "If you truly don't care about a person, it's indifference—not anger—you feel. I know."

"You don't know anything! I'm not angry...not the way you think! I despise Dan for what he did to me...to my career...not for any silly emotional reasons."

"Just what did he do?" probed Trent.

Carla's chin lifted, her eyes narrowing. "Dan Wright double-crossed me."

"Tell me about it."

Trent said the words softly and she felt the anger drain from her body. Why, she didn't know, but suddenly she did want to tell Trent everything. "Dan and I met over a year ago. We were both manager trainees. Actually I'd been in the program for some time before Dan started. He was assigned to me as a part of his training.''

It seemed easy to recall how she'd felt when she first met Dan. "You saw how good-looking he is. Mr. Adonis. The tellers used to flock around him, bring him coffee and run errands for him. Some even typed his paperwork. It used to irritate me, but Dan took it for granted. He could have had any woman he wanted. That's why I was surprised when he asked me out.''

"Why should you be surprised? You're a beautiful woman,'' Trent interrupted.

"Then beauty is truly in the eyes of the beholder because it's not, as I've told you, an attribute that's been assigned to me before. Oh, I know I'm not ugly, but really, most men do see me as neat, intelligent or efficient—not beautiful. And I've never cared. I've never wanted men to think of me as a sex object.''

"Dan didn't think you were sexy?''

Carla laughed, thinking back on her relationship with Dan. "Hardly. Our first date turned into a private tutoring session. After that we went out sporadically. He has a way of making people think he's up on everything, but Dan has some real problems grasping the banking business. I'd say at first he saw me strictly as someone who could help him.

"Not that I cared,'' Carla defended. "I enjoy talking business and Dan was genuinely interested in mastering the bank's procedures. And I'd be a fool to say I didn't like having a man as good-looking as Dan squiring me about town, taking me to dinner and plays.''

"But after a time the two of you fell in love?''

Trent finished his wine and set his glass aside.

"I'm not sure if what I felt was love. We were comfortable together. We were equals—or so I thought. One day we discussed getting married and the idea sounded fine to me.

"However, Dan didn't want to finalize our engagement until he talked to Thorton Wood. Not that the bank has any policy against married couples working together, but Dan insisted."

She grimaced. "I don't know whether it was a blessing or a bane, but Wood was pleased with the idea. He said we were the perfect match. So we announced our engagement. But it disturbed me that Dan had needed Wood's approval."

"Dan doesn't sound like a man carried away by his emotions," observed Trent, his fingertips moving lightly over her arm.

"We bankers are a conservative lot," she stated, defending herself as much as Dan.

"I know one who has some fiery emotions." A lazy figure eight traced on the soft inner flesh of her arm sent flames shooting through her and Carla jerked her arm away.

"Please don't." Carla eyed him warily, remembering how she'd reacted to him the night before. "A bank officer cannot indulge in emotions. People don't want a sybarite handling their money." Without thinking, she rubbed her arm, trying to erase the feel of his touch.

"If you say so," Trent grinned. "Why did the engagement end, if you two were such a perfect match?"

"It was the manager's position ... downtown. When it opened, I told Dan I was going to apply and he had a fit. He expected me to step aside, let him have the job."

"But you didn't."

"No, I didn't. I wanted that job. I'd worked hard for it and I was far more qualified than Dan was. Why should I have stepped aside?"

"You shouldn't have," Trent easily agreed. "What happened? Did your ambition disturb Dan?"

"Disturb him?" She laughed, finding it amusing for the first time in months. "Dan told me I should be backing him, not trying to hinder his career. He didn't understand at all that I also had a career, that I needed his support."

"So you went your separate ways and you hate him because he couldn't understand your ambition...your needs."

"No, that isn't why. I could accept that I threatened him. But when Dan realized I wasn't going to withdraw my application for that job, he stabbed me in the back." Carla bit her lower lip, the anger once again surfacing.

"What happened?" Trent asked softly, slipping his arm around her shoulders.

"He lied." She took in a deep breath. "He was so damned afraid I would get that job, he told Wood that I had a heart problem, that I was under a doctor's care and that the stress of being a manager would be too great for me."

"You have a heart problem?" Trent's eyebrows shot up, and Carla suspected he was seeing her as a weak, sickly woman—just as Wood had.

"No, not really," she hurried to explain. "If I drink coffee or anything with caffeine in it, my heartbeat becomes arrhythmic. Dan knew that was all it was. He was with me when the doctor gave me the results of my tests. If I stay away from caffeine, I'm fine. After I found out what Dan had said, I went to Wood and explained the situation. But it was too late. By the time I got a doctor's statement, giving me a clean bill of health, Wood had already announced that Dan would be the new manager of the downtown office."

"And you were given the Roseville job as a pacifier?" Trent accurately surmised.

"More or less. Wood had to give me the next manager's position that opened up and Roseville was the one."

"All right, so you're bitter about what Dan did to you—and with justification—but deep down... honestly... how do you feel about the guy? Do you still love him?"

"No," Carla said truthfully, without hesitation. "I loved what I thought he was, but that was just a facade. He taught me one thing though. Now I realize, if I want to succeed, make it to the top, I'm going to have to do it on my own."

"Oh, Carla," Trent murmured, tightening his hold around her shoulders, "you see yourself as a conservative staid banker, but inside of you there's a warm giving woman. There's room for love in your struggle to the top. What you need is the right man to stand behind you."

Carla laughed self-consciously. Sitting up straighter, she pulled away from his embrace. "I suppose you're now going to tell me that you're that man?"

He grinned as he watched her nervously run her fingers through her hair. "Who knows? I liked what I saw last night."

"Last night was not me," she said, color flushing her cheeks as she remembered how irrational her behavior had been. Reaching forward, she picked up their empty wineglasses and set them back in the picnic basket. "I really think we should go now. It's getting late and I have that housework to do."

"Don't tell me you're going to let this beautiful lake go to waste?" Trent asked, stopping her from picking up the empty wine bottle.

"I never should have agreed to come this afternoon." Already he knew more about her than most people. It was unnerving how he affected her.

"I'm going for a swim," Trent stated, rising from the blanket. "It's been almost an hour since we finished eating and that water looks inviting."

"Fine, you go swimming, I'll clean up." He wasn't going to change her mind this time.

She expected him to argue, but he didn't. As she stacked the cardboard containers in the basket, she was aware that he was undressing, but she kept her eyes on her work.

"Actually, it's only fitting you're cleaning up," Trent called to her as she tossed in the last napkin and brushed crumbs from the blanket. "Women are innately domestic. I'm sure being out in the fresh air like this, surrounded by so much beauty, is of little interest to you. You'd probably far rather be home cooking, cleaning and sewing."

"If you believe that, Mr. Campbell," Carla muttered, sitting back on the blanket and wiping beads of perspiration from her brow, "then you don't know me at all."

But when she looked up Carla knew from his grin that Trent was only teasing. He'd stripped away her excuse to leave by baiting her with chauvinistic rhetoric. And she'd taken the bait.

Still, she knew she couldn't stay. The sight of him, with nothing on but a pair of brief black swimming trunks turned her limbs to rubber. Light-brown hairs covered his forearms and legs, a thick golden-hued mat across his chest tapered down to a thin line that disappeared beneath the waistband of his swimming trunks. His appearance aroused a primeval response in her and Carla hurriedly looked away.

"Are you changing into your bathing suit or do I throw you in with your clothes on?" he challenged.

"You wouldn't dare," she gasped, glancing back. The glint in his eyes warned her that he might. Rather than chance a physical confrontation, Carla relented.

Quickly she slipped out of her tennis shoes, chinos and blouse. She removed her dark glasses and placed them beside her purse, then tossed her head, her long hair brushing her back. "All right, Mr. Campbell, you've called the shots so far, but beware, this woman is about to invade your territory."

"It could be dangerous," he taunted, a subtle sensuous undertone to the words.

"I've never been one to back off from a challenge." Especially from a man, she might have added.

Trent watched her come closer, his eyes raking over her slender figure, pausing for a moment at the full curve of her breasts. "You know, my dear feminist, you really are beautiful."

To her surprise, he turned his back to her and walked into the lake. Carla watched him swim away, his strong arms easily cutting through the water. It was evident Trent was a good swimmer.

Taking time to allow her body to adjust to the water's cool temperature, Carla looked around. It was beautiful. A slice of paradise. There was a peacefulness to the area. Birds sang, squirrels chattered and frogs croaked. Even the fisherman, his boat looking so small in the distance, seemed to fit into the scheme of nature.

The sun beat mercilessly down on her back, but Carla didn't notice. Her attention had been caught by a silvery-blue dragonfly. Gracefully it hovered above the water's surface, its gossamer wings catching the light and turning iridescent.

"I made it. Think you can?" Trent called.

Tearing her eyes away from the dragonfly, Carla looked out over the shimmering water. Trent had swum the distance across and was standing knee deep, not far from the opposite shore. It wasn't a particularly wide lake; still she hadn't done any swimming in years.

"I'll come back, if you think it's too far," he yelled.

Now, *that* was a challenge. "If you can make it, so can I!" she shouted and splashed into the water.

She was less than half-way across when Carla knew she'd overestimated her abilities and underestimated the distance. Too many hours behind a desk had left her out of shape. Her arms were tired and heavy, her right leg cramping. "Trent!" She cried his name as the calf muscle knotted and a sharp pain shot up her thigh.

"Hold on," he yelled, making a shallow dive and swimming toward her.

"My leg," she gasped, then went under. Panic

gripped her as she sank into the dark cold depths. Flaying her arms, she resurfaced.

"Relax! Try to float," Trent ordered, closing the gap between them.

Carla did try, but her leg wouldn't cooperate and she only managed to swallow a mouthful of water. Choking, she tried to tread water, but any amount of movement brought instant pain to her right leg. Her arms were tiring. The water seemed to be pulling her down.

"You're a fighter," she remembered her dad telling her when she was only six. "A chip off the ol' block." Funny how that childhood memory popped into her mind. With a renewed effort she fought to keep her head above water.

"Take it easy." A steellike arm wrapped around her waist supporting her, as Trent sculled with his other hand. "I've got you."

"My leg," she moaned, the solid strength of his body buoying her up. "It's cramped. I can't move it."

"Then don't try. Just relax and let me do all of the work."

Carla was aware of her total dependency on Trent. Scared and helpless, she let him tow her toward shore. Fear turned to embarrassment, then reproach. How stupid she'd been, taking up his challenge. She should have known better.

Trent paused, catching his breath, and Carla wrapped her arms around his neck and clung to him. "I haven't been swimming for years," she confessed, pressing her ashen face against the hollow of his neck and shoulder. "I shouldn't have tried to make it that far."

"Then why did you?" he demanded. "Watching you go under took ten years off my life."

"Because you implied that I couldn't."

"See the trouble being a feminist will get you into."

"I'm not a feminist!" *Damn, he was irritating.*

"You're certainly feminine." Trent pulled her close, so that her breasts, covered only by the thin nylon of her bathing suit, pressed against his chest. "You have a nice figure, Miss Parker. All the right curves in all the right places."

Her toes touched the slippery, slimy bottom of the lake and Carla realized Trent was standing. She tried to take a step away from him, but he only hugged her closer. "Trent, don't...please." She kicked her feet, hoping to find a more solid foothold, but her action merely sent a quick, sharp pain tearing up her leg. Realizing she was in no position to fight, she tried words. "You're embarrassing me."

"I didn't think feminists got embarrassed," he grinned, watching the color come back into her cheeks.

"Proof that I'm not one."

"Ah, but you believe women are equal to men, don't you?"

"I believe women should have an equal opportunity. There's always the matter of individual ability." He had clearly demonstrated his superiority to her when it came to swimming.

"I like a woman who has confidence in herself," Trent said. He took a few steps toward shore, carrying her with him, then stopped. "I like a woman who isn't afraid to voice her opinion or accept a challenge."

No words were spoken as they gazed into each other's eyes, yet an understanding was developing between them. Even though she could now stand, Carla made no move to leave. *He isn't threatened by me*, she thought. An inner confidence, something intangible, but very real, gave him strength. She knew that, just as clearly as she knew Dan was weak. She also knew Trent didn't want to dominate her, that he was willing to accept her as an equal.

"Trent, I think we'd better get out of the water. I'm getting cold." Her voice was no more than a whisper.

"Can you walk?" he murmured, brushing her wet hair back from her face. "Or would you like me to carry you?"

"I can walk." She had to walk. If she didn't, in a minute she would be telling him how wonderful he was, kissing him, making a damned fool of herself.

One step was all she managed. Her calf-muscle cramped; she involuntarily cried out and Trent gathered her into his arms. It happened so quickly, Carla didn't have a chance to think or to object.

"I'm sorry," she apologized, wrapping her right arm around his neck, her left sliding behind his back. "You've already done so much and I know I'm no lightweight."

"I hadn't noticed."

His smile was warm, his eyes gentle. Carla lowered her gaze and leaned her head on his shoulder. He *was* strong. She could feel his muscles rippling beneath her fingertips, the cords of his neck tightening against her arm. Water was dripping from his hair onto her body, blending with the droplets on her skin. It took all of her willpower not to caress his shoulder with her lips and taste him.

Gently he lowered her onto the blanket, then went to get their towels. Shivering, she quickly rubbed herself dry. "Now, let's take a look at that leg," he said, kneeling down in front of her.

"It's just a cramp...a charley horse," she told him, cautiously touching the knotted muscle with her fingers.

"Ohh," she cried out, tears springing to her eyes when he reached forward and gingerly began to rub the painful area.

"You've got to relax it. Lie back and let me do the work."

She did, biting her lip to keep from crying. Methodically Trent worked his fingers over the area, gradually warming and relaxing the muscle. Through half-closed eyes Carla watched him, the pain easing, then disappearing. Her breathing was deep, her chest slowly rising and falling as her entire body fell under the hypnotic spell of his gentle massage.

When his hands stilled, her lids flickered, then slowly opened. He was watching her, his lambent gaze expressing a hungry longing, and Carla felt her stomach muscles tighten. Her entire body was responding to that look, a fiery warmth spreading between her legs, her breasts swelling, nipples hardening. He could see the change. He had to know how he was affecting her.

"Carla, I know I promised—" he rasped, his eyes meshing with hers.

She tried to be rational, but her body had a will of its own. Without saying a word, she raised her arms and he came to her. His lips were cold, but they warmed quickly as he plied kisses to her mouth. Carla ran her fingers lightly over the smooth skin of his shoulders, down his back and up again. He felt so good to the touch, so warm and alive.

"I don't know what it is about you," she moaned, as his mouth left hers to trail kisses over her face. "I promised myself this morning that this wouldn't happen again."

"I made myself the same promise," he breathed near her ear. His hand covered a breast, his palm lightly massaging its fullness, and she groaned.

With an easy flick of his fingers, her bathing suit was lowered, her breasts exposed to his view. "Beautiful," he murmured, his hands caressing soft creamy flesh, his fingers tracing the circle of each aureole.

When his mouth once again claimed hers, his lips relayed a yearning she shared. He wanted all of her, and willingly, eagerly, Carla surrendered to his persuasive assault. Her fingers raked through his damp hair, then spread out across his broad back. He was a man and she wanted to be the woman to satisfy his needs. It was crazy, it was irrational—and it was wonderful.

Even minimal clothing seemed a barrier. She groaned in satisfaction when he moved closer, the hairs on his chest brushing across her breasts, his thighs pressing against hers. He was fully aroused and the feel of him excited her. Seductively Carla slid her hands down over the silky material of his swimming trunks to capture his bottom in her palms. Slowly she twisted her hips in an age-old dance and heard him suck in his breath.

Her actions were motivated by a strange, over-powering drive that she barely understood, while Trent skillfully made love to her, knowing exactly where to touch—and when. She closed her eyes as his tongue flicked in and out, finding the sensitive pulse point at her throat, then dropping to the valley between her breasts.

And as his lips moved lower, so did his hands. Her breathing was rapid, her body quivering with excitement when his fingers grazed the material between her legs. Then he shifted his body lower, drawing one nipple into the warmth of his mouth, encircling it with his tongue, wetting it completely.

Her body ached to surround him, just as he now surrounded her. She groaned out his name and he understood, his lips returning to hers, his loins rubbing slowly and seductively over her hips.

Time was meaningless. His tongue delved deep into her mouth in a slow, provocative gesture, then she reciprocated, tasting him, probing. He caught her tongue between his teeth, gently but forcibly holding it before slowly letting her slide it out. Symbolic and erotic, the act left her breathless. There was no question of their mutual desire. Trent moved his hips across hers, his legs pushing her knees farther apart. Only the material of their bathing suits separated them. Carla slid her fingers under the waistband of his trunks, easing them lower.

A thudding, splashing sound filled her ears. She was drowning in ecstasy. Caught in a whirlpool of emotions, she was swirling in an eddy, about to go under. Then suddenly Trent stiffened.

"Pull up my swimming trunks," he rasped, raising his head.

"Why?" She ached for him, needed him. Couldn't he understand that?

"My trunks," came his sibilant order. There was another splash.

Carla obeyed, only beginning to understand. Trent leaned back and with a jerk of his hand, yanked up the front of her damp swimming suit, managing to cover both breasts in the single movement. Again Carla heard a thud, then a splash—this time closer. Trent rolled off her and grabbed the nearest towel, wrapping it around his waist. His body blocked the lake from her view, but Carla understood now. The fisherman was rowing toward them.

"Howdy folks," an old man's voice called. "Nice day for a picnic, ain't it."

"Certainly is," Trent returned, his cordial greeting giving no clue to his emotional state.

Carla quickly glanced down at her front, hoping she looked halfway presentable. There was nothing she could do about the flush of her cheeks, but a quick brush of her fingers through her hair put it in some semblance of order.

"You're new around here, ain't ya?" the old man asked, stepping out of his boat with a splash.

"Just visiting. Neil Higgins told me about this lake. Can I give you a hand?"

"Sure can, mister," the fisherman answered. "If you'll hold the boat, I'll go get my car. It's easier to load her if I can just back right in."

Carla recognized the voice and wished she could shrink her five feet ten inches down to the size of an ant. In a moment Trent would no longer block her from his view and Seth Harcort would see her.

Trent rose and grabbed the rope the old man

tossed him. It was only then that Seth recognized her. "Why, Miss Parker, I didn't know you was here."

"How are you doing, Seth?" she asked in a voice she hoped sounded calm. "Catch many fish?"

"Mess of them, Miss Parker." The old man's blue eyes, magnified by thick glasses and sunken in a tanned, weathered face, were filled with curiosity as he glanced from her to Trent and then back again. "Uh...I'll go get the car," he stammered, shuffling off toward the Chevy.

"That was close," Trent called to her, holding onto the boat as the old man started his car and began to maneuver the boat trailer back toward the water.

"Too close," Carla groaned.

"I don't think he saw anything." Trent combed his fingers through his hair, smoothing its tousled look.

"I think he suspects we were doing more than getting dry."

"That so?" Trent grinned, then stepped out of the way as Seth backed the trailer into the water.

While Trent and Seth loaded the boat, Carla pulled on her clothes, then finished packing the picnic basket. By the time the men had the boat securely tied down, she had the area cleaned and the blanket refolded.

"Sure you won't take some of these fish?" Seth asked, when Trent returned to Carla's side. "Make you two a nice supper tonight."

"He's not staying for dinner. He's.... We're...." Carla stopped, not quite certain how to explain her relationship with Trent to Seth.

"What she's trying to say," Trent intervened, "is that we're eating out this evening. Thank you for the offer, but unless Carla wants a few for her freezer, you'd better keep them."

Carla shook her head.

Seth slung the pail back into the boat, then ambled toward his car. "See you two around then. Got to get home for chores."

"So do I," Carla reminded Trent, as the Chevy and boat bounced out of view.

"No more hanky-panky?" he teased, watching her cheeks color.

Carla turned away and walked back toward the picnic basket and folded blanket. "I don't know what happens to me every time you're around."

"Whatever it is, I like it," he murmured, coming up behind and kissing her bare shoulder.

"Trent!" She gasped as his hands wrapped around her, encompassing her breasts.

"Don't worry, honey. This time we're alone."

"This has got to stop!" she protested, placing her hands over his and trying to wriggle free of his grasp.

"Why?" he demanded, turning her so that she faced him. "I like holding and touching you. And you feel the same way. Don't deny it."

Gazing into his velvety eyes, Carla knew it was the truth. "Yes," she sighed, shaken by her own admission. "But it's wrong."

"Why?"

"Trent, this can go nowhere." She pushed herself out of his arms, shaking her head.

"It almost went quite a way."

She was all too aware of how far they had nearly gone. "Another five minutes," she groaned.

"And our fisherman would have had more than a fish story to tell. All right, honey, I'll take you home, but you're wrong. We're headed somewhere. I know we are."

By the time Trent had dressed, Carla had twisted her hair back behind her ear and once again looked cool and efficient. For a while they said nothing as they drove back toward Roseville, then Trent reached across the console and took her hand in his. "There's an old business friend of my father's in Fort Wayne. I promised to have dinner with him tonight. Will you go with me?"

Carla knew she couldn't. She needed time to sort out her feelings, time to try to understand what was happening to her. "Not tonight," she responded, hoping he would accept her excuse without an argument. "I have that vacuuming to do and clothes to wash."

"I'll help with the vacuuming. You'll like Ed. He's in his seventies, but as sharp as a tack and as spry as a kid."

"No, please," she insisted. "Give me a rain check."

"A rain check or an escape?" Trent frowned, his dark glasses once again hiding his eyes from her view.

"Could I escape?" she asked, wondering herself at how quickly he'd captured her interest.

"Not without a struggle. All right, you can meet Ed another time. Tonight you wash and iron, but tomorrow you're mine."

"I always go to church on Sundays," she told him.

Not that she expected that to dissuade Trent. Already she'd learned he was persistent to a fault.

"Fine. The Claytons invited me to dinner. Henry wants to show me around the farm. I'll call and tell them to expect us after church."

5

ALL HEADS TURNED toward them as they entered the church. Carla led the way down the aisle, Trent close behind. As she slipped into a pew, she tried to ignore the curious stares, but under such close scrutiny it was difficult to maintain a poised mien. Trent sat down beside her, and Carla automatically reached for a hymnal, then studied the directory at the side of the church for the number of the opening hymn.

"We're being watched," Trent whispered, his leg brushing against her thigh.

"They're curious. I've never come to church with a man before."

"I'm honored."

"Wait until you've sat through one of Reverend Morrison's sermons before you say that," she chuckled under her breath.

Later Carla had to admit it was one of the Reverend's better sermons. Not that she paid her usual close attention to what the gray-haired minister was saying. Church was not the appropriate place to be feeling sexy, but every time Trent's leg touched hers or his jacket sleeve rubbed against her arm, a mindless craving curled deep inside of her.

Most of the hour was a blur. She remembered standing beside Trent, singing the old, familiar hymns, the deep resonance of his voice filling the air, and she remembered Trent taking her hand in his, their fingers entwining as they bent their heads in prayer. But that was all. Despite Carla's good intentions, Reverend Morrison's words about a better life became confused with memories of an afternoon by a lake and what had followed.

To her surprise, Trent had insisted on helping her with the housework. "I promised," he told her. "Now, where's the dust cloth?"

"You've got to be kidding." She hadn't believed for an instant that he was serious.

"I suppose you're going to tell me that real men don't do housework." He sighed in mock resignation. "That's the problem with you feminists. You stereotype us, then are disillusioned when we break out of the mold."

That was enough. Carla found Trent a dust cloth and put him to work. If he wanted to impress her with his domesticity, fine. She'd take all the help she could get. Besides, maybe seeing him involved in such a menial task would lessen the erotic effect he had on her.

But Carla discovered Trent looked just as virile picking up a piece of colored depression glass and wiping it clean as he had in his bathing suit. She was relieved when he glanced at his watch and announced that he'd have to be leaving. Relieved and a little disappointed. She knew if he kissed her again, as he had at the lake, they would end up in her bedroom. Therefore, when Trent left her with no more than a peck on the cheek and a promise to pick her up for church, she had felt unfulfilled.

Still, Carla was glad she hadn't given in to her physical longings. She didn't yet accept her feelings for Trent and until she did, it would be better to proceed cautiously.

Cautious, prudent Carla. She smiled as the minister gave the final benediction. She certainly hadn't been prudent at the lake. No telling how much Seth Harcort had seen or would tell others. She would just have to hope Seth's eyesight was as poor as he said, and that Trent's body had blocked most of their activities from view.

After church many of the congregation came over to say hello. The younger women seemed most eager to meet Trent, and Carla didn't blame them. Dressed in a light-brown sports jacket, trim brown slacks, a cotton shirt, tie and leather shoes, he stood out among the other men in the church.

Shaking Reverend Morrison's hand, she introduced the two men, then waited as the minister offered Trent his usual greeting. At last outside, Carla looked quickly over the slowly dispersing congregation. "I hope Bob Dolman hasn't left. I tried to get his attention inside, but he was busy talking."

"Carla," a strong, high-pitched voice called from behind them, "you must introduce me to your nice young man."

Although the color rushed to her cheeks, Carla managed to remain poised and unruffled. With a smile, she turned to greet her neighbor. "Miss Atherby, how nice you look this morning. I'd like you to meet Trent Campbell. He's thinking of buying the Clayton farm."

"Do say," commented Cora Atherby, extending a frail, wrinkled hand.

"I've seen you out tending your flowers. You have

a lovely garden, Trent said, taking her nand in his and smiling warmly.

"Why, thank you." The old woman eyed Trent closely, the blue of her eyes bright and alert. "Have you known Carla long?"

"No, not very long, but sometimes it seems like forever. I do like your dress, Miss Atherby. Rose is your color."

He certainly knew how to flatter, Carla decided, watching Miss Atherby melt under Trent's charm as easily as the younger women had. "Oh, there he is," Carla cried, spying Bob Dolman on the edge of the lawn. "Excuse us, Miss Atherby, but I need to talk to Bob before he leaves."

Leading the way, Carla guided Trent through the groups of chattering churchgoers and caught the president of the Rotary Club just as he reached his car. "Bob, do you have a minute?"

Bob Dolman was nearing fifty, built on wiry lines, and balding. His grocery store in Roseville was thriving and most of the town's businessmen looked to him for leadership. "For you, Carla, always," he smiled as she approached.

"Actually, it's not for me—directly," she began and introduced Trent. "Trent is thinking of buying the Clayton farm. There's a possibility he might be bringing one of his companies to Roseville and he'd like to talk to the Rotary Club. Think it could be arranged for Monday?"

"This town could use some new industry. What kind of business are you in?" asked Bob, giving Trent a closer look.

"Campbell Industries is involved in a variety of products, from tiny electronic circuits to dishwashers," explained Trent. "One of our existing plants needs to be moved to a spot where there's more potential for growth. From what I've seen, Roseville may be the right location. But, before I make a decision, I'd like to talk to the town's economic leaders. Carla suggested the Rotary Club meeting might be a good time and place."

"I think we could work you into the agenda," Bob said, nodding.

Carla noticed Trent had carefully avoided mentioning the chemical plant, per se. His evasiveness disturbed her. He'd said he didn't want rumors to spread before he had a chance to present the facts, but could there be something he was trying to hide?

"If you'll excuse me," Bob said, glancing at his watch, "we have guests coming this afternoon and I have a lawn to mow. Sue is already upset with me because I was at the golf club all day yesterday."

Trent shook the man's hand, commented on the heat of the day and casually slipped his arm around Carla's shoulders. "We'll see you Monday, then."

"If you move Baker Labs here, will there be chemical waste?" she asked, as they slowly walked back to her house.

"Some. That's one reason I'm taking soil samples and getting drainage reports. I have no desire to pollute the environment. Our modern-day technology produces these toxic side effects, and I feel it's our responsibility to see to it they're disposed of in the safest possible way. Baker Labs maintains standards far above the legal requirements. We wouldn't have it any other way."

"What about air pollution? Would there be a smell?"

"Occasionally, but nothing too repugnant."

Carla took in a deep breath of clean air and felt her first qualms about Baker Labs coming to Roseville.

"I noticed a strong aroma coming from the barns on the Clayton farm," Trent said, reading her concern. "Wouldn't you call that air pollution?"

"I guess so." She smiled as they strolled up the walk to her house. The smell of the barns was always with Henry Clayton.

"Now do you see why I don't want to say anything until Monday? The fears you have are exactly what others are going to have. Nowadays all chemical plants have a stigma attached to them. Everyone wants the products, but no one wants a plant in their backyard."

"Because of what's happened in the past. Look at Love Canal," argued Carla.

"I'm not saying there isn't reason for concern. The people in Roseville have a right to know that Baker Labs isn't going to ruin the land or drive them from their homes. What I want to do is quell those fears, get the facts out before the rumors begin."

"But will you give us the facts?" Carla had been about to open her front door, but she stopped and turned to stare at Trent. What did she know about this man, anyway? Really know?

The look he gave her was pleading. Tentatively he reached out to touch her face. "Carla, I've always been honest with you. That, you have to believe."

She trembled slightly. Logically, as a businesswoman, she knew she should be wary. Facts, not emotion, should sway her judgment. But reason seemed immaterial. Deep inside Carla was certain

Trent was an ethical individual and that she could trust him. "I do believe you," she whispered, never drawing her eyes away from his.

His fingertips brushed across her cheek, seductively stroking her smooth skin. His gaze held her prisoner, restraining her with invisible bonds. Captivated, Carla couldn't move and slowly Trent lowered his head.

"I forgot to ask—" a high-pitched voice called from across the street.

Flustered and embarrassed, Carla stepped back from Trent and turned to look over to where Miss Atherby stood. The gray-haired woman smiled and went on. "I was wondering, Carla, if you could help with the church bazaar in August?"

"Certainly, just let me know where and when," Carla answered, her cheeks flushed.

"Maybe your friend would like to help?"

Carla glanced at Trent, then told Miss Atherby, "I don't think Mr. Campbell will be here in August."

"Does that mean you won't be buying the Clayton farm, after all?" asked Miss Atherby, staring at Trent.

"My plans are still up in the air, but if I'm here for the church bazaar, I'll be glad to help."

"Good, I'll count on that." Her heels clicking a sharp staccato, Cora Atherby strode up her walk to her house and Carla returned to the task of unlocking her front door.

"Privacy seems to be a rarity in this town," stated Trent, following her inside.

"Living in Roseville is like living in a fishbowl. What should I wear this afternoon?"

Slowly Trent let his eyes travel over the back of

the white cotton sundress she'd chosen for church. "You look lovely just as you are."

She'd left her hair down that morning. Why, Carla wasn't sure, other than she knew Trent liked it that way. What she didn't realize was, with her hair cascading over her shoulders, the image of the impenetrable banker was broken. And when she turned to face Trent, he saw a very desirable woman.

The slight vee of her dress's neckline gave a hint of the full curve of her breasts, the fitted bodice accented her slender feminine form and the slightly flared skirt flattered her hips. She could read the desire in Trent's eyes even before he took the step toward her. "Don't, please," she whispered, her legs locking and refusing to move.

"Don't what?" he murmured, his hands grazing her bare shoulders, his fingertips seductively playing along the strap that tied around her neck.

"Don't kiss me." The beat of her heart was erratic.

"Why not?" he asked, lifting a finger to trace the outline of her mouth.

"Because we always get carried away." Her throat felt dry, the words sounding far too husky to be natural.

"And is that so bad?"

His mouth captured hers before she had a chance to reply. Firmly he held her, one hand moving slowly down her back, sending shivers along her spine. *You can't let him do this!* her mind cried, but she only sighed when he caught her lower lip between his teeth and gently tugged on it.

His jacket felt soft beneath her touch and she worked her fingers around to his chest, where her hands slid under the lapels, to spread across the front of his cotton shirt. *Lime*. That's what he smelled like this morning. Lime and soap, and a distinct male scent that was all his own.

She groaned as his lips moved over hers. Every inch of her face was thoroughly kissed, every corner of her mouth investigated. And when his tongue slid past her teeth—so tantalizing in its leisurely investigation—she responded with a thrust of her own.

"Oh, Carla," he moaned, kissing her neck, one hand moving around to stroke the edge of her breast.

It was happening again, this crazy, uninhibited yearning he could so easily ignite. Carla struggled to control the desire building in her. Another minute and she would be melting in his arms, begging him to take her upstairs and make love to her. Opening her eyes, she forced herself to look out through a window. This was Roseville, Indiana—not a fantasy land.

"Stop," she groaned, pushing her hands against his chest, trying to escape the intangible hold he had on her. "I have an important position in this town. I can't be seen as...as a—"

"Woman?" he offered, only slightly loosening his grip. "And why not, Carla?"

"I have a reputation to maintain. In a few weeks you'll be gone, but I have to live with these people...work with them." No longer was she physically struggling.

"Is it your reputation that's bothering you or my leaving?" he asked, drawing her against his chest so that her cheek rested on his shoulder.

"My reputation, of course," returned Carla, knowing she couldn't tell him he was becoming far too important to her, that if he made love to her he would possess her, body and soul.

Pulling out of the circle of his arms, she walked over to the banister, using its solid strength for support. "Trent, this is a small town. People around here have old-fashioned ideas about what is proper and what isn't. Didn't you notice the way Bob Dolman looked at us when you put your arm around me? He read it as more than just a casual gesture. And if Seth tells what we were doing yesterday—" She sighed. "Maybe it would be better if I didn't go with you to the Claytons'."

Trent shook his head. "Is this the way you handle all of your dates? Do you always make promises, then back out?"

"No, of course not, but under the circumstances—"

"Under the circumstances I suggest you go freshen your lipstick. I'm not leaving this house without you."

"Trent, you don't understand," Carla feebly protested, afraid another afternoon with him might be her undoing.

"Mrs. Clayton's expecting you. When I called her yesterday and told her who I was bringing, she was delighted. What would she think if you didn't show up?"

"You're manipulating me again," Carla groaned, torn between wanting to be with him and her fear of the consequences. "You do it every time I say no to you."

Trent closed the distance between them, and catching her chin with the tips of his fingers, forced her to look at him. "Carla, if I'm manipulating you it's because you force me to. Tell me what you want and I'll do it. Just come.''

"No touching while we're there," she demanded. "No arm around my shoulders...or waist. No holding my hand."

"Can I look at you?" he asked, an edge of sarcasm to his voice.

"You're not taking me seriously."

"Oh, but I am. You'll have to excuse me, honey, but I'm not used to dating a feminist. I haven't learned all of the ground rules."

"I am not a feminist." She was beginning to hate that word.

"Aren't you?" His thumb gently caressed her cheek and he stared at her face for a long drawn-out moment, then nodded. "All right, Carla. No touching while we're at the Claytons'. You're the bank manager, I'm the land buyer. As far as the citizens of Roseville will be concerned, we're friends and nothing more."

AND THAT WAS THE WAY they explained their relationship to Henry and Mary Clayton. Mary, with her warm homey smile, rosy plump cheeks and amply rounded body, seemed disappointed, but her husband, Henry, took it in stride—that is, if he understood any of the explanation. His lack of hearing was a drawback to any conversation.

Carla was always amused when Henry and Mary came into the bank. From the confines of her office she could hear Henry, his voice loud and clear, and Mary, repeating everything the teller said at least once and sometimes twice. When she had to deal with him, Carla always made certain everything was in writing and that Henry read it. It saved a lot of repetition and problems.

"Glad you could come," Mary was saying, leading Carla to the kitchen as Henry steered Trent outside, toward the milking barns.

Carla noted the automatic division of the sexes with a knowing smile. With the older farmers it was accepted that the women would prepare the meal while the men discussed "business." It was a tradition based more on necessity than bias. Someone had to cook and tend the children and someone had to plow the fields and milk the cows. Even modern conveniences hadn't entirely eliminated those realities.

"Not that I don't enjoy having men over," continued Mary, "especially when they're as nice looking as that Mr. Campbell. But I do get tired of hearing farm talk. All Henry seems to do lately is complain about milk prices."

"Can I help you?" Carla offered as they stepped into the steamy kitchen. The rich aroma of beef came from a pot on the stove and a pile of red-skinned potatoes sat near the sink. "Where's your peeler?"

"Why, thank you," said Mary, pointing to a drawer under the counter. "But don't you dare get that lovely white dress dirty." Digging into another drawer, Mary pulled out a pale-blue cotton apron with delicate cutout and embroidered flowers across the pockets.

As the two women worked, peeling potatoes, chopping cabbage and slicing cucumbers, they talked about gardening, the weather and the price of groceries. Occasionally Mary gave a pan of green beans a stir, checking their dull green color. "Picked them this morning," she told Carla. "They should be good and tender by the time we sit down to eat."

So much for *al dente*, Carla mused, knowing the beans, cooked for hours with strips of bacon, might be lacking in vitamins, but would be rich in flavor. "How's your new granddaughter?" she asked, remembering she'd read in the local paper that the Claytons were grandparents again.

As Mary boasted about all of her grandchildren, Carla stared out the window. Trent was following Henry across the yard, dust now covering his highly polished expensive brown shoes. It had to be at least eighty degrees Fahrenheit outside, and not a cloud visible in the sky. Trent had removed his jacket and tie and unbuttoned the top two buttons of his shirt. Henry, in his faded bib overalls and worn cotton shirt, was talking, pointing to the three tall blue silos next to the main barn.

Watching Trent, Carla felt a knot form in her stomach. But her interest went deeper than simple physical attraction. Trent emanated an aura of desirability. It wasn't anything one could see or touch, but it was there, just as real as his ready smile and warm handshake. And it drew her to him, pulled her closer every minute they were together. He fascinated her, preoccupied her thoughts and held her under his spell—and that frightened her. She couldn't be falling in love with him. That wouldn't be logical.

"Mind putting these on the table?" Mary asked, drawing Carla's attention back from the two men outside and away from her thoughts. The older woman held out a stack of inexpensive plates with a flower pattern, and Carla took them, smiling her answer.

The table was set in the midwestern farm tradition—everything on at once. Steaming bowls of potatoes and vegetables and the platter of meat were set next to dishes of cole slaw, gelatine salad and sliced tomatoes. There were this year's dill pickles, cucumbers soaked in cider vinegar, carrot sticks and celery. Hot gravy was placed near the homemade biscuits and Carla poured cold tea into tall glasses filled with ice. No wine with this meal. Alcohol and long afternoons of work did not mix.

The heat in the kitchen had dampened Carla's skin, and her hair stuck to her neck. *If I'd been more practical and worn my customary knot instead of leaving my hair down for him, I'd be cooler,* Carla mused, wondering if she'd lost all sensibility since meeting Trent. She was brushing a lock of hair back, away from her face, when Trent and Henry entered the house.

"Showed him all the barns and stock," Henry announced to his wife as he stepped out of his boots and proceeded in stockinged feet to the sink to wash up. "Now he's got a good idea of what he's gittin'."

Trent stood in the doorway, his eyes on Carla. Leisurely, lovingly, his gaze traveled over her flushed face, down her front to the embroidered apron, then back up again. Neither Henry nor Mary seemed to notice, but Carla did. Trent's look took her breath away. Like a gentle caress it brushed over her body, lingering at her breasts, stroking her hips, stating his desire as loudly as any words.

"I didn't know feminists wore aprons," he said softly.

"If they're practical, they do," Carla murmured back.

"Damn, it's hot out there," Henry exclaimed, wiping his brow as he pulled out the chair at the end of the table and sat down. "Sorry, Miss Parker. Didn't mean to use profanity in front of a lady, but I declare, this is the hottest July we've had in years. If we don't git some rain soon, we're going to have problems. Real problems."

"I'm sure Carla and Mr. Campbell are well aware of the temperature and lack of rain," Mary interrupted, sensing her husband was about to go into a long dissertation on how the crops would fare if it didn't rain. "Sit down, sit down," she ordered, motioning to both Trent and Carla.

Trent held Carla's chair for her. It was a simple gesture, but one that made her self-conscious, and she quickly glanced at the Claytons, wondering what they thought of Trent's attentiveness. But Henry was already serving himself spoonfuls of mashed potatoes and Mary was scurrying between the table and the kitchen, getting the last of the food onto the table.

"You promised—no touching," Carla whispered as Trent sat down beside her.

"And what's wrong with helping a lady with her chair?" he asked, innocently raising his eyebrows as he reached for the bowl of green beans.

"You know what I mean. The way you looked at me when you came through the door. They're going to suspect."

"Suspect what?" Trent teased, his arm brushing against hers as he held the dish for her to take a helping. "I was merely admiring . . . your apron." He grinned.

"We always say grace," Mary stated, finally seat-ing herself across the table from Carla and Trent. "You give the blessing, Henry."

Heads bent, neither Henry nor Mary noticed Carla's shocked expression when Trent slid his hand over her hip and along the ruffled edge of her apron. "Amen," he said as Henry ended the blessing. Carla's mouth shot open to voice a protest, but found her words stopped by a carrot stick.

"Don't say anything you'll be sorry for," Trent warned under his breath, his brown eyes dancing with amusement. Remember your reputation." Looking across the table, he raised his voice and said to Mary, "I've been admiring this apron Carla's wearing. Did you make it?"

"Why yes, I did," she replied, obviously surprised to have a man comment on her sewing.

"Very nice. The embroidery is Italian cutwork, isn't it?"

"That's right, but how did you know?" She was beaming as she passed Trent the biscuits.

"When I was a boy I broke my hip and had to stay in bed for three months. I've always been very active and I hated the confinement, so my mother used to sit in my room with me to keep me company. When she wasn't helping me with my homework, she would do her embroidery. One day I asked if I could learn, and she taught me some of the basic stitches and showed me the different styles of cutwork.

"I learned to make French knots, but never mastered the little picots you've used here. I always twisted the thread around the needle, or whichever way is wrong." Casually he reached down and fingered the fine open work in the apron, caressing Carla's thigh in the process.

From her side of the table Mary couldn't see the way Trent's fingers lingered on Carla's leg. "The open areas do give it a nice texture," agreed Mary. "I won first prize at the county fair with that apron."

"Lovely," Trent murmured, sending Carla a sidelong glance.

Her skin tingled where his fingers rested, and a hot pulsing fire, which had nothing to do with the outside temperature began to burn deep within her body. She reached for her iced tea, needing something to cool her. Trent's hand moved farther down her leg, and Carla smiled as she thought of another use for the cold liquid.

He was taunting her, teasing her, arousing her even as they sat at the table, and there was nothing she could say to him without bringing attention to what he was doing. Half angry, half amused, Carla lifted the glass, then intentionally let her hand tilt to the right. Liquid and ice spilled across Trent's lap, over the exact location she'd aimed for. *That should cool him off.*

Trent gasped and pushed back his chair with a scraping sound. As he stood, the ice fell from his lap to the linoleum. Mary also jumped from her chair, rushing to the kitchen to get a towel. Henry merely laughed and Carla had to fight back an impulse to join him.

"I'm so sorry. Can I help?" she asked, trying to sound contrite.

"Acccidents do happen," Mary said, handing Trent a dish towel.

Trent dabbed at the front of his pants, removing the excess liquid. But he was watching Carla, whose eyes were dancing. She knew it was no accident—and so did he.

She hoped the tea wouldn't stain his slacks, but his shocked expression had been worth the penalty she would have to pay...sometime. As he pulled up his chair and sat down again Trent eyed her with a half smile. Carla pretended to ignore him—even tried to give the impression she was reloading her weapon as she poured herself another glass of tea. But she knew she'd never dare repeat that trick. A smile from her then one from him, guaranteed, at least temporarily, a truce.

Henry hadn't missed entirely the unspoken exchange. His bushy white brows rose curiously and he rubbed his chin with a gnarled hand before reaching for another biscuit. "You got a wife, Campbell?" he asked, pouring gravy over the biscuit.

"No, I'm not married," Trent replied, looking away from Carla.

"Man needs a wife." Henry studied Carla for a moment, and she busied herself with her food, hoping he wouldn't make any rash judgments. One thing she didn't need was another person gossiping about Trent and her.

To her relief Henry changed the subject. "This chemical plant you're planning on bringing here, will it be very big?"

"Yes," Trent nodded.

"Too big to be built and still leave the farm as is?"

"I'm afraid so," Trent answered. "You'd be surprised how many acres a chemical plant the size of Baker Labs takes up. Besides the buildings, there will have to be parking for the employees and land for waste disposal."

Carla looked up. "What kind of waste disposal?"

"We'll have to build a treatment plant to purify the water before it's released back into the environment, and all of the solid waste will be stored here, on site. Don't worry—" he smiled at her "—there won't be any pollution. You can check our past record if you don't want to take my word."

She would check. Not because she didn't trust him, but because she would want facts—statistics— to quote if she was asked her opinion. Trent had requested that Henry and Mary not say anything to anyone about Baker Labs for a few days, but Carla knew questions about environment safety were sure to arise at the Rotary Club meeting.

"You have any boys?" Trent asked Henry.

But he didn't hear the question and Mary answered, "We have two boys. The youngest one, John, is twenty-eight and Adam is—" she paused a moment "—will be thirty-five next month."

"If you'd like the farm kept intact, why not sell t one of your sons and let him run it?"

"Sun? Comes up 'round six a.m.," Henry answered glancing out the window.

"No, father, he's talking about our sons...Adam and John," Mary nearly shouted. "He wants to know why we don't sell the farm to one of them."

Henry's brow wrinkled and a sad look filled his wizened blue eyes. "They don't care nothin' about this farm. Don't like the long hours, they say. Or the dirt and smell. I ask you, what's wrong with gittin' up early and workin' close to nature? Bet they don't get as much satisfaction at their jobs as I do seein' a calvin' or knowin' I've given hundreds of school children the milk they need to grow."

"Calm yourself," Mary soothed, patting Henry's arm affectionately. Then she looked at Trent and Carla. "Henry still gets upset with the boys. Adam moved out to California and works with one of those computer companies. John's in Indianapolis. He has his own little printing company. Neither of them ever wanted to be farmers, not even when they was little. Now Henry's getting too old to farm, so we've got to sell. I'd like to see the farm stay as is as much as Henry does, but things don't always work out the way we like. Your offer was a good one, Mr. Campbell. If you have to tear the ol' place down, you have to." But she looked wistfully around the room and her brown eyes became misty.

"You understand I have to make certain the land is suitable before the sale will be complete, don't you?" Trent was speaking to both of them, but it was Mary who heard and nodded.

"If it's all right with you, I'm going to come by tomorrow morning and take samples of your water and the soil."

"Water?" Henry frowned. "Water's checked twice a year. Has to be 'cause of the milk. Our water's okay."

"I'm sure it is, but I'd like to have our labs run some tests," Trent insisted. "We look for different things than the state might."

"Good water here," Henry went on, rising from his chair to go into the kitchen and draw a glass of water from the tap. "Finest well water 'round."

"You come out tomorrow, and I'll see to it you get your samples," Mary smiled.

Trent drank the glass of water Henry brought back to the table, complimented its taste, then rose to help Mary clear dishes from the table.

"The women can do that," Henry stated, side-tracking Trent before he could return for a second load. "I don't think you realize what a valuable piece of farmland this is. Despite the dry weather, I've got the best corn crop in years. Come with me."

He gave Trent little choice. Stuffing his stockinged feet back into his dirty rubber boots, the old farmer hustled his guest out of the house, rambling on about bushels per acre and record yields. Carla was left in the kitchen with Mary.

And for once in her life she was thankful she'd been relegated to kitchen duty. Henry was leading Trent toward a dented, rusted red truck that had seen far better days. One window was cracked, its shocks were long gone and the left fender was held together with baling wire.

As the old vehicle bounced and wove down a dirt road that passed the barns and cut through a field of corn, Carla picked up a dish towel and grinned. Poor Trent. He certainly wasn't going to have a very comfortable ride. A point to consider. Hot and dusty as it was, Trent might not be very affable by the time he returned.

But if his tour of the farm was less than pleasant, Trent didn't say anything when he stepped out of the truck. And a smile still came easily to his lips when Mary offered him a tall glass of lemonade. What did look the worse for wear were his pants. Dust had clung to the area where the iced tea had wet the material and had turned the color a darker shade of brown.

She was staring at the stained pants, feeling guilty about her impetuous move at the dinner table, when she realized where she was looking and that Trent was watching her. Immediately her cheeks turned red and she looked away.

"Oh, dear, your trousers are soiled where that tea was spilled," exclaimed Mary, age allowing her the grace to discuss the problem openly. "Come inside and I'll see what I can do about it."

"Carla and I really must be going," Trent said, consulting his watch. "Thank you for the offer, but I know a way to take care of the problem."

He looked at Carla and smiled, and she swallowed hard. What he had in mind, she wasn't certain, but the end of the truce was drawing near.

"Before you go, you must take a few tomatoes," insisted Mary. "We picked a basketfull this morning."

She went back into the house before either Trent or Carla could object and returned a few minutes later with a grocery sack filled with homegrown vegetables, including vine-ripened tomatoes, prickly cucumbers, shiny green peppers and big red onions.

"Thank you for everything," Trent said as he took the bag, then shook hands with Henry. "I'll see you tomorrow."

"What'd he say?" asked Henry, looking to Mary for his answer. "Something going to seed?"

As they drove away from the Clayton farm, Trent was laughing. "First thing Henry needs to do, after selling that place, is buy himself a hearing aid. They're quite a couple. Did you see all the food Mary put in that bag? There's enough to feed a family of eight."

"She had enough food on that table this afternoon

to feed an army." Immediately Carla wished she hadn't mentioned dinner. Trent's sidelong glance and half smile told her he had his revenge planned.

"Well, thank's for a lovely day," she said, opening the car door as soon as he stopped in front of her walk. "I'll see you tomorrow at the meeting."

For a second she thought she might make it inside her house before Trent realized what she was doing. Then she heard his car door slam and his call. "Haven't you forgotten something?"

She turned to face him. She would apologize for the stain but nothing more. It was, after all, half his fault.

"You have the refrigerator, not me," he said, coming toward her carrying the sack of vegetables.

She'd completely forgotten the food the Claytons had given them. Carla reached for the bag, but Trent ignored her gesture and walked past her to her front door.

He had something in mind. But what? Nervously she fumbled for her key. By the time she managed to unlock and open the door, Carla had made up her mind that there was no way she was going to let Trent into her house. If it came to an argument— well, he could just take the bag of vegetables.

But, to her surprise, he handed over the sack without a protest. "Well...thank you again," she mumbled, stepping inside.

"There's one thing more." Trent smiled, stopping her before she could close the door.

"What?" The glint in his eyes was enough to tell her the truce had ended.

"You owe me one pair of clean pants."

"What do you expect me to do, buy you a new

pair on a Sunday afternoon in Roseville? It was an accident." She dared him to contest her statement.

"Don't you clean up after accidents? It won't take long. They're wash and wear. A half hour in the washing machine, another half hour in the dryer, and they'll look like new. I certainly can't walk into the hotel looking like this."

The spot was in an obvious place, and she could understand his wanting something done about it. "Perhaps you could carry your jacket in front of you," she suggested lightly.

"Perhaps I could sit out here in my underwear and discuss the weather with Miss Atherby," was Trent's response. Reaching down, he unbuckled his belt.

At the mention of Miss Atherby's name, Carla's eyes went to the house across the street. The woman wasn't in sight, but there was no telling where she might be or how much she could see—or hear. It angered Carla to know that Trent had picked up on her sensitivity to Miss Atherby's reaction. He was manipulating her again, and she saw no way out. As he reached down to unzip his trousers, she pushed open the screen door for him to come in. "The bathroom's upstairs. I'll wash your damn pants as soon as I get these vegetables into the refrigerator."

By the time she climbed the stairs, Trent was taking a shower, his cheerful whistle rising above the sound of running water. He'd piled his clothes neatly outside the bathroom door, including his undershorts, shirt and socks, as well as his trousers. "Now he expects me to be his maid," Carla grumbled, picking up the dusty, dirty clothes. The smell of cow barn lingered on the material and she wrinkled her nose. She didn't blame him for wanting every-thing washed, but he could have at least asked.

And you would have refused, she honestly admitted to herself.

Downstairs, in the laundry room off the kitchen, Carla used a spray to loosen the dirt on the front of his trousers. In minutes, Trent's clothes were being gently agitated in warm, soapy water. He was com-ing down the stairs when she stepped into the entry-way. His hair was wet, but neatly combed; a few drops of moisture still clung to the hairs on his bare chest, and an oversized dark-blue velour bath towel was wrapped around his hips. He reminded her of a Scotsman in a kilt. Only there was no question in her mind as to what he wore under his makeshift skirt.

"I feel better," Trent proclaimed. "Hope you don't mind my using the shower. I have a friend who's always talking about getting out of selling stocks and into farming, but it certainly wouldn't be my choice of occupations."

"Your clothes are in the wash," Carla informed him. Every inch of him was virile male, and know-ing only a simple twist of material kept that towel in place made her uneasy.

A crazy yearning was growing in her, the sensa-tion starting at the pit of her stomach, weakening her limbs and confusing her. She wanted to touch him—rumple his wet hair, caress his body, and feel the play of his muscles beneath smooth, clean skin.

Embarrassed and shocked by her thoughts, Carla turned away and walked into the living room. Quickly she went to the windows and closed the draperies. It certainly wouldn't do for Miss Atherby to see Trent wandering around the house nearly naked.

Trent stood in the doorway, watching her nervous actions. "Any ideas on how we can entertain ourselves until I have some clothes?" he asked, a suggestive intonation to the words.

Carla gulped. "How about watching television?" She stepped to the set and pushed some buttons, flipping from channel to channel.

"I don't want to watch television." Trent's husky voice startled her. He'd come up silently behind her and now his fingers covered hers as he turned off the television.

Carla jerked her hand back as if nipped by an electrical shock. He was so close she could smell his clean manly scent, and her desire to reach out and touch him grew even more intense.

Slowly she backed away from the television, away from Trent, afraid she might give in to the impulse. But he followed like a panther stalking its prey, his eyes enticing, his smile inviting. A bookcase stopped her retreat and Carla took a deep breath. She just couldn't... it wouldn't be right... not for her.

"Perhaps you'd like to read," she suggested, handing him the first book her fingers touched.

Amused, Trent's eyebrows rose, *"How to Make Love to a Man,"* he read from the cover.

"It isn't.... I couldn't have..." Carla gasped, grabbing the book back out of his hands.

He laughed.

No such title met her eyes. It was a book on nutrition, and if she'd been less agitated he never would have fooled her.

Trent took the book from her hand and slid it back

into place on the shelf. "You should read the chapter on beating the jitters."

"I am not jittery," insisted Carla, slipping away from him and going over to the stereo system.

"Aren't you?" He was behind her again, his fingers lightly touching her shoulders, his voice low and seductive.

Carla trembled. It would be so easy to give in, turn around and melt into his arms. Instead she picked up a tape and slipped it into her cassette player. "You like jazz?" she asked, trying to sound blasé.

"Some," he murmured, pushing her hair away from her neck and blowing softly into her ear. "Tell me what you like, Carla."

Oh, please, she silently screamed, his warm breath igniting a fire deep in her loins. *Give me strength.*

"I...I like Chuck Mangione and Pat Metheny." Her voice quavered.

She moved away from Trent, trying to make her escape seem casual. His hands slid down over her arms, exciting every nerve ending, but he made no attempt to stop her.

Lyrical, rhythmic music filled the living room as she wandered toward the couch. Suddenly Carla wished she hadn't chosen the Pat Metheny tape. The music had a romantic sexual undertone that only added to the primitive urges she was already battling.

"Not bad," commented Trent, smiling when she glanced back to see if he was following her. "Personally I like George Benson and Al Jarreau."

Carla stopped by the couch and turned to face Trent. "I have a few George Benson tapes, if you'd rather play one of them."

"This is fine. You know, it's nice to know we have more than one passion in common."

He walked slowly toward her and Carla's eyes involuntarily darted down to the towel, then back up. He smiled knowingly and the color rushed to her cheeks. Her entire body felt feverish.

But Trent looked cool and comfortable. He stopped in front of her and lightly touched her arms with his fingertips, tracing little invisible circles on her bare shoulders. "I think we have many things in common," he said, his voice low and husky.

His gaze was intense, his brown eyes threatening to consume her. Warm, gentle fingers moved down her arms, to her waist and then up, over her breasts. His thumbs brushed against her nipples and each bud hardened to a peak. Another second or two and he would kiss her and Carla knew it would then be too late, that her resistance would be gone.

She stared at him, trembling. It would be so easy to give in, let herself be carried away by the uninhibited emotions simmering within her. But she didn't dare. Not with Trent. With him it would be more than just a casual affair.

"How about a game of checkers?" she blurted out, desperate for any escape. Before he could move, she grabbed the checkerboard from the end table and placed it on the coffee table.

"Checkers?" mumbled Trent, his frustration evident.

"It's a great way to spend an afternoon. But I must warn you, I used to play for hours with my father and few can beat me."

"Checkers," Trent repeated, then sighed and sat down on the rug in front of the coffee table, making certain the towel covered him. He studied Carla as she emptied the playing discs out of the box onto the board, then smiled and reached for the blacks. "It's not exactly what I had in mind."

She hurried to set up her players, not certain if she was relieved or disappointed that he'd agreed to her suggestion. *Fickle female,* she chastized herself. *You want him to seduce you—but you don't want him to. One of these days you're going to have to make up your mind.*

"Your move," he said, and she pushed a center player forward into battle. At some point she would have to face him—and her feelings—but not now, not this afternoon.

The first game was a testing of abilities, a planning of strategies and counter strategies. The long evenings she'd spent playing with her father had taught her the subtleties of the game, but it seemed Trent was also an astute player. She barely beat him the first game.

"Very good," he nodded, setting up the board for a second game.

"Thank you. Most people underrate the game of checkers. They think of it as child's play and I find them easy to beat. You're pretty good, though," she acknowledged.

"From you, I take that as a compliment." He stretched, his muscles rippling as he flexed his shoulders. Then he leaned forward to study the board. "You were very close to your father, weren't you?" He moved a center piece diagonally to the right.

"I still am." Her mind was already three moves ahead.

"No brothers? Only the sister you mentioned?"

"Right." Carla looked up from the board, trying to

analyze Trent's line of questioning. "Diane's three years younger than I am. Why?"

"Just curious."

He moved and she suppressed a smile. "You're going to lose, you know."

"I wouldn't bet on it. You don't like to be bested by a man, do you?"

"Not particularly." She slid her checker into place. "Your move."

He touched his man, hesitated a moment, then pushed it exactly where she had planned. She jumped him, only to realize he'd maneuvered her into a trap. Two of her reds went to Trent.

"You're trying to keep me from concentrating, that's what you're doing." It was obvious she'd have to watch him more closely.

"Carla short for Charlotte?"

"No, long for Carl. I was named after my grandfather."

"And the initial J stands for?"

"Jayne," she chuckled, moving her man to a position she knew would trap Trent. "My father's name is Jay. It was all planned out. Either way they could use grandpa's and dad's names. But dad was very disappointed that I wasn't a boy."

Now, why had she told him that? Her eyes flicked up to catch the sparkle in his brown gaze. It seemed she was always telling him more than she intended. "I think I'd better toss your clothes into the dryer," she said, rising to her feet. "Don't cheat while I'm gone."

"I never cheat," he grinned, holding her eyes with a level stare. "If I win, it will be fair and square."

She knew he wasn't talking about the game of

checkers. It was her body he wanted. He was playing by her rules, at least for now, but he had her at a disadvantage. Win or lose, he wouldn't be hurt. To him she was one of many. Whereas, for her, the stakes were higher. Her body could not be taken without sacrificing a piece of her heart. That was what she had to face.

Her pulse was racing as she pulled his wet clothes from the washer and tossed them into the dryer. A quick check revealed the spot on Trent's trousers was gone. Soon he would be gone, too. Not just today, but forever. That was why she couldn't let down her defenses.

Carla returned to the living room, determined to whip the pants—or, in Trent's case, the towel—off him. But every time she thought she had him cornered, he turned the tables on her. For every black she took he gained two reds. Soon she conceded the game and they started a third.

As she studied the board trying to devise a new game plan, Trent rose and went over to the stereo to play the other side of the tape. Carla smiled when he settled back down across from her. Despite the tension there was something very comfortable about spending an afternoon playing checkers and listening to music. She was just beginning to relax when Trent jumped her man then looked up and asked, "Have you ever made love to a man?"

"Of course." She met his gaze directly.

"Then why all these games, Carla? I know you want to."

"What I want and what's good for me aren't necessarily the same." She looked down and reached for a red disc.

"It would be good." His hand covered hers, stopping her before she could make her move, and Carla trembled.

"Please, Trent, just give me a little more time."

For a minute he said nothing, then he nodded, smiled and lifted his hand. "All right, a little more time. But I warn you, Miss Parker, one of these days I'm going to carry you off to your bedroom and I think you'll find what you want and what's good for you are one and the same.

SHE EXPECTED HIM to leave once his clothes were dried and he'd dressed, but instead he went straight to her refrigerator and began to pull out its contents. "I'm starved," he said. "We should be able to make something out of all of this." He looked over the array of vegetables the Claytons had given them and her miscellaneous leftovers. "You want to do the honors, or shall I?"

Carla raised her hands and stepped back. "Cooking is definitely not my forte. Go to it, chef."

He did, with an ease that amazed Carla. Trent washed and drained the lettuce, peeled and julienned vegetables and began to put together a delectable-looking salad. Meats and cheeses added protein, herbs the seasoning. As he worked, Carla watched and occasionally handed him an ingredient or two.

"Did your mother also teach you how to cook while you had that broken leg?" she finally asked when Trent began to mix the vinaigrette dressing.

"No. My uncle, my mother's brother, is the one responsible for my interest in cooking. Whenever I went to his house, he and I would concoct a new recipe to spring on my aunt." Trent laughed. "My poor aunt never knew what to expect. Actually, most of the time what we made came out quite well, but we did have a few failures. One of these days I'll cook a proper meal for you."

"This one looks great," said Carla, pulling out silverware and mats to set the table in the dining room. "Frozen dinners are my usual fare. I bless the man who invented the microwave."

The dining room was dark, but the coolest in the house. The antique dropleaf table, buffet and china cabinet had come from an estate auction, the straight-backed chairs from a yard sale. Carla rarely used the room, but Trent's salad seemed to warrant more ceremony than the Formica-topped dinette in the kitchen. Impulsively she added a candle to the setting and opened a bottle of white wine. Carla was pouring the wine when Trent entered the room proudly carrying his chef's salad.

"Perfect," he nodded, placing the bowl on the table. "Madame, dinner is served."

He held her chair for her, his hand brushing softly over her shoulder as she sat down. Carla looked up, but he merely smiled then went around to the other side of the table.

They talked, they laughed and they ate. It was an enjoyable meal. And after dinner they washed and dried the dishes together. Carla was actually disappointed when Trent said he had to leave. "So soon?" came out before she realized what she was saying.

Wickedly he winked at her. "I could be talked into spending the night."

Before she could say anything, he kissed her, his mouth possessively claiming hers, his arms going around her until she was molded to his form. A word of protest formed on her lips, but he merely took advantage of the opening to bring his tongue into play. Earlier frustrations flamed back into passions and a moan of submission escaped from deep within her. Then, to her surprise, he pulled back.

"I'll see you tomorrow," he whispered and was gone.

6

THE TELEPHONE RANG. Carla reached for it automatically, her concentration remaining on the article in the *Wall Street Journal*.

"What are you trying to pull, Carla?" Dan snapped over the line. "He's Trent Winston Campbell, vice-president of Campbell Industries, entrepreneur and industrialist. Certainly no dairy farmer."

"Why, Dan, hello, and how are you, too," Carla sweetly returned, ignoring his sarcasm.

"I'd be a hell of a lot better if I knew what was going on."

A smile of satisfaction curved Carla's lips and she leaned back in her chair and pushed her reading glasses back up on her nose. Evidently Dan had discovered Trent's identity, but not why he was in Roseville. She could imagine Dan's blond eyebrows puckered above those pale blue eyes and the frown that would be marring his good looks. "I wasn't aware that you were so interested in what was going on in Roseville," she responded, keeping her tone very professional.

Dan swore. Carla was certain he must be alone in his plush office, the door closed. The thought of him sitting behind the desk that should have been hers, his name beneath the title on the door, rankled her.

"Watch it, Dan," she warned, "or your blood

pressure will go up. And you know how Wood feels about heart problems."

"You're avoiding the issue," Dan growled. "What is Trent Campbell doing in Roseville?"

"Right now, probably visiting the dairy farm he's buying. In an hour, taking me out to lunch. Is there a message you'd like me to relay?"

"You know as well as I do a man in Trent Campbell's position doesn't buy a dairy farm—at least not for the purpose of milking cows. Something's going on there, Carla, and I'm going to find out what it is."

"It's a free world," she coolly stated, wondering how long it would take Dan to learn about Baker Labs. Not that it mattered. In a few more hours Trent's plans would be public knowledge.

"Come on, Carla." Dan had changed his tack, his voice pleading. "For old times' sake, what's Campbell doing there?"

"As far as I'm concerned, there are no 'old times,' Dan. And if Trent wanted you to know why he was in Roseville, he would have told you Friday night. As it is, I'm not at liberty to divulge that information."

"It has something to do with the bank, doesn't it? That's why you won't tell me. Does Wood know?"

The edge was back in Dan's voice and, though his frustration amused her, Carla was tiring of the conversation. "No, Wood doesn't know, but as soon as the Indy State Bank is involved I'll see to it that Wood has all the information he needs. Now, if you'll excuse me I have work to do."

"You want to impress Wood, don't you? You want

a promotion. You've never forgiven me for beating you out of this job.''

Calmly, but firmly, Carla said, ''We both know how you got that job. Unlike you, Dan, I don't go around trying to impress people all the time. When Trent wants it known why he's here, both you and Mr. Wood will find out...just like everyone else. Now, goodbye.''

Hanging up the receiver, Carla stared at the wall. It was ridiculous to let Dan upset her, but he had. What a fool she'd been for having once thought she loved him.

Finally she managed to set aside her anger and her attention returned to the newspaper. *Fed Lowers Discount Rate.* That would help profit margins. *Gold Prices Up; Dow Jones Down.* Trent was probably getting those soil samples now. The thought darted through her mind, interrupting her analysis of the business news.

All morning that had been happening. At the strangest times Trent's image or memories of things he'd said or done would creep into her thoughts. She'd tried to concentrate harder, but it was useless. Trent seemed to be a part of her every breathing moment.

He'd called her early that morning before she left for work. His voice had sounded so good and she'd readily agreed when he suggested picking her up at the bank and taking her to the Rotary Luncheon. Since then, time had dragged and she'd caught herself looking at the clock far too often. Forcing herself not to think of him, she finished her perusal of the paper.

Trent arrived just before noon. "Is Mr. Parker in?" he asked, tapping on the open door.

"Déjà vu?" Carla laughed, putting down a loan application she was checking and taking off her glasses. "Did you get those samples from the Clayton farm?"

"Mission accomplished, with the help of Mary. I'm afraid there's still a communication gap between Henry and me." Trent closed the door and walked across the room to her desk.

"Dan called this morning," Carla told him, as she stood and straightened her slim beige skirt. "He knows about Campbell Industries."

"But not about Baker Labs?" Trent's glance skimmed over her tailored outfit, lingering a bit longer on her white silk tie-blouse. The delicate material clung to the curve of her breasts, delineating their fullness and giving a faint view of the lacy camisole she'd slipped on that morning.

"He'll find out soon enough, but by that time everyone in town will know."

"I've missed you," Trent murmured. Taking her into his arms, he kissed her long and thoroughly.

Surrounded by his strength, Carla knew reality was far better than memories. Only three days before, he'd stepped into her office and into her life. Now he seemed an integral part of her. His lips touched her forehead, his fingertips caressing her back through the fabric of her blouse.

"I missed you, too," she sighed. It was the first time she'd admitted the fact, even to herself. And, when his mouth covered hers a second time, she responded with a natural, giving warmth that readily grew until it was Trent who pulled away.

"Honey, a few more minutes of this and I'm going to suggest we forget that Rotary meeting in lieu of something more satisfying."

"And what possibly could be more satisfying than lunch and a stimulating afternoon with Roseville's finest?" His kiss had shaken her and she hoped a little teasing would ease the sexual tension between them.

"Hmm. I can think of one activity that would be very satisfying, but that I want to pursue at my leisure."

Cheeks flushed, Carla turned away, her hands going up to check if her hair was still neatly arranged in a knot. It was.

Trent chuckled. "You're blushing again."

"You're impossible," mumbled Carla, but a little smile curved her lips and her cheeks were bright as she walked to the door. "Considering we have a luncheon in ten minutes, don't you think we'd better get going?"

The Roseville Rotarians met downstairs at the local church. Every week the Women's Auxiliary prepared and served a well-balanced, delicious meal, and Carla always looked forward to these meetings. Today she felt even more exhilarated knowing Trent would be speaking, and she wondered how her fellow townspeople would react to his proposal.

Trent paused before entering the room, buttoned his dark-brown sports jacket and straightened his tie. "Ready?" he asked as Carla double-checked her own appearance.

"Ready."

She barely had time to introduce Trent to each of the Rotary Club members before lunch was served.

The church women moved quietly from table to table, bringing to each person a salad, home-baked rolls hot from the oven and small dishes of butter.

Trent conversed easily with Leonard Klein, the local contractor, who was seated next to him. He briefly mentioned Baker Labs, but it was Leonard who monopolized the conversation. Construction around Roseville had been down for years.

The ladies removed the salad bowls and replaced them with the main course—slices of pot roast, mashed potatoes covered with thick brown gravy and portions of tiny sugar-sweet peas. Then came wedges of homemade pie, that were downed with gulps of strong hot coffee—with the exception of Carla, who had her usual glass of milk.

When the dishes were cleared, Bob Dolman stood and called the meeting to order. Trent was formally introduced just before the end of the meeting.

Briefly he describe Campbell Industries and his job, then he got down to specifics. "Baker Labs manufactures a variety of chemicals, some of which I'm sure you've used, either in your homes or on your farms. We're proud of our record of excellence. In the past five years the company has shown amazing growth with profits to match. It has grown so much, we need a new location for the plant. Your town—Henry Clayton's farm, to be specific—is our choice."

The eruption that followed Trent's statement took Carla by surprise. Jim Taylor, who owned the feed and grain mill just outside of town, was objecting loudly.

"We don't need another Love Canal here in Roseville," he stormed, his round face growing red above his faded blue collar. "I'll do without your damn chemicals before I allow you or any other fast talker to come in and turn my home into a garbage dump." Shaking his fist, Jim glared at Trent.

"Jim!" cried Bob Dolman. "Let's hear the man out."

"I can appreciate your concerns," Trent said calmly, making eye contact with as many of the men present as possible. "Roseville is a lovely town and a perfect place to raise a family. But let me assure you, Baker Labs would neither turn this area into another Love Canal nor into a garbage dump. The safety standards of Baker Labs are stringent."

"That's what they thought in Michigan. Now they've got PCBs." Jim was on his feet again.

Carla was impressed. Even under fire Trent remained poised and unperturbed. His attitude alone had a calming effect on those present. With several loud raps of his gavel and a warning to Jim, Bob reestablished order.

As Trent explained the environmental precautions exercised by the chemical plant, Carla glanced around the room. Felix Gordon was taking notes. Undoubtedly he'd write up something for his newspaper. This would be the biggest story to hit the Roseville *Sun* since those two teenagers from Fort Wayne robbed Bob's grocery store. The county sheriff had arrested them before they'd gotten fifteen miles out of town.

Ken Pierce, the hardware store owner, looked interested in what Trent was saying. Often enough he'd mentioned the need for more industry in Roseville and Carla was certain he'd welcome the coming of Baker Labs. In fact, most of the men present—she was the only woman beside those working in the kitchen at the meeting—seemed interested. Jim Taylor was the exception. He was still flushed, Trent's words of assurance doing little to mollify him.

"Just how large a chemical plant is this?" Bob asked when Trent had finished talking.

"Baker Labs now employs a thousand workers. I foresee an expansion to two thousand after we move."

Herb Swanson, who owned the lumber mill, whistled. "You should like that, Leonard. Lots of houses to build."

"With your lumber, no doubt," Leonard Klein hooted back. Any increase in new homes would help both men.

The dissenters were in the minority, most objections being issued by Jim. As the men in the room began to recognize the benefits to their places of business, new questions arose and Trent carefully answered each thoroughly and thoughtfully.

"HOW DO YOU THINK IT WENT?" asked Trent, as he walked with Carla back to the bank.

"They were definitely interested," she told him happily. "I knew they would be. For the last six months all I've heard is how Roseville's economy needs a shot in the arm. Jim Taylor was the one who surprised me. He deals with chemicals every day. I would have thought he'd be more objective."

"He did get quite emotional once or twice. Actually there were fewer objections than I'd expected. On the whole, I'm quite pleased. I liked those men. They asked in-depth questions and were quite receptive."

A few scattered gray clouds covered sky. The temperature seemed far more comfortable than it had been in weeks. Whether it was the effects of the cooler weather or of Trent's good humor, Carla didn't know, but impetuously she said, "Come to dinner tonight."

"At your house?" His eyebrows rose mockingly. "For what, frozen entrée à la microwave?"

"Don't knock it until you've tried it," she returned, pushing open the glass door to the bank and leading the way to her office.

"I wouldn't think of doing such a thing." He grinned, his eyes raking over her slender figure making Carla wonder if they were discussing the same subject.

Trent closed the door behind him as he followed her into her office. Reaching forward, he caught her hand, stopping her progress toward her desk. Pulled against his solid chest, Carla laughed, trying to ignore the warm tempting sensations surging through her. Toying with his gold collar pin, she fluttered her long lashes in mock surprise. "Why, Mr. Campbell, whatever are you doing? You did follow me in here to discuss a loan, didn't you?"

"What's the going interest rate?" he teased, his face only inches from hers.

"Quite high."

He closed the gap, his lips on hers. For a long drawn-out moment he savored the kiss, then hugged her close and sighed. "You drive a hard bargain, Miss Parker. Will you accept a deferred payment?"

"A what?" she mumbled, nearly purring as he pulled off her earring and nibbled on the lobe of her ear. Pressed against his body, she could feel the hard length ot him, the taut muscles of his arms and the angles of his hips.

"A rain check," he explained, his hands working over the back of her blouse, sliding it from her skirt until his fingers slipped beneath the silky material to touch her camisole. Apologetically he gazed down into her lambent green eyes. "I have to fly to Philadelphia this afternoon with those samples I took from the Clayton farm."

Her disappointment was more intense than she liked to admit, but a smile covered her feelings and she managed a quip about his leaving. "Anything to get out of eating my cooking, right?"

"Feminists can't cook. Didn't you know that?" he laughed, lightly kissing the tip of her nose.

"A feminist can do anything she likes. That's what makes her a feminist." The defiant tone she once might have used was missing. Trent made her feel soft and feminine—but not weak.

"I have a feeling you can do many things very well," he murmured, giving her one last hug before letting her go.

"When do you expect to be back?" Her voice cracked, and she cleared her throat. Going to her desk, she tucked her blouse back into her skirt and tried to regain her composure. No sense getting emotional. It wasn't like he was leaving for good.

"This should be a short trip. Mainly I want to get those lab reports and talk to my father, let him know what I've found here."

He'd be gone just a day or two, but already Carla felt an emptiness she didn't like. Studying his broad shoulders the rich color of his hair and the casual assurance of his stance, she wondered how one man could have infused himself into her life so quickly.

"Well, people have told me they'd do anything to avoid my cooking, but none have ever gone as far as Philadelphia." She had to keep the conversation light or she knew she'd make of fool of herself.

To her relief Trent laughed. "Maybe we'd better leave the cooking to me. Now, give me a kiss and send me on my way, before I decide to take a later flight."

Carla didn't need to ask what would happen if he did take a later flight. His smile was message enough. "Get out of here," she ordered, trying to sound serious. "If half the town hasn't already seen you kissing me, I'll be lucky. Don't forget, this is Roseville, Indiana—fishbowl, U.S.A." A nod toward the window reminded him they could be seen with very little difficulty.

Despite her protest, he kissed her—gently, tenderly, and for a very long time. "Don't forget me while I'm gone," he murmured, his hand sensuously stroking her back. Then he went to the door. But he paused before he left, winked and tossed her earring back to her. "We'll talk more about that interest rate when I return. Take care, Carla."

MORE THAN ONCE that afternoon she caught herself daydreaming, looking at a loan application or mortgage papers, but seeing Trent's face, remembering that last lingering kiss. Dinner time wasn't any better. Taking a soufflé from the freezer and popping it into her microwave reminded her of his teasing comments about her cooking.

She'd never been a good cook. Maybe because her mother was. Cooking, to Carla, had always been "woman's work"—a term she hated. Oh, she could handle the basics—boil water, scramble an egg—but something always seemed to go wrong when she tried to cook. Either the meat was burned, the vegetables turned soggy, the potatoes didn't cook through or the rice was sticky. The truth was, in the kitchen she was a disaster.

Sitting at her table, picking at her food, Carla was disturbed by the melancholy that filled her. For years she'd lived by herself. Eating alone wasn't anything new and it had never bothered her before. But tonight something seemed to be missing—or someone.

As evening turned into night she tried to read a book, but after starting the same page three times, gave up and put it aside. The television had nothing to offer and music only reminded her of Trent. Funny that he should also like jazz. She wondered what other interests they had in common. He certainly wasn't a bad checkers player.

The rain came that night. A soft, nourishing shower that would bring new life to the land. For a while Carla stood at the screen door, watching the street turn shiny under the street light. Then she locked the doors and went upstairs.

In a hot steamy bath she leaned back and half closed her eyes. Her mind was reeling, emotions colliding with pragmatism. What she needed was time to think—time to straighten out her feelings.

She was a practical woman, used to making decisions based on facts. All of her life she'd weighed the pros and cons of every situation. Always she looked to the future, considered her career, then took the most logical step to bring her closer to that goal.

Even accepting Dan's proposal had been a carefully analyzed decision. She had assumed what she felt for Dan was love and that he loved her. Hindsight showed she was wrong, but at the time she'd had no way of knowing Dan had lied to her and would lie to Wood.

But what about Trent? What did she feel for him? And could she trust those feelings?

It was impossible for her to explain her reactions whenever Trent touched her. Even the sound of his voice was warm and soothing. And now this emptiness, this yearning for him to return. It frightened her.

She couldn't be in love with the man. It didn't make sense. She'd only known him three and a half days. No, it couldn't be love.

Carla sank deeper in the tub, the water covering her breasts like a warm caress. An image of Trent flitted through her mind and a tingling sensation radiated from between her legs. Even her stomach did a little flip-flop at the thought of him. She sighed and resigned herself to the truth. She did love him. She loved him and missed him and logic had nothing to do with her feelings.

Perhaps they had known each other only a short time, but during those hours they'd spent together Trent had shown her he was a sensitive, giving man, perceptive, honest—even humorous. He accepted her as she was and, as he'd said, she didn't frighten him. With him she felt complete, alive and totally female. She didn't fear being dominated by him. Just the opposite. With Trent she felt freer to be herself than ever before.

But knowing she was in love with Trent only

complicated matters. There was no future for them.
It was folly to think he might also be in love with
her. He was a mature, experienced man, who undoubtedly met many women he was attracted to
during his travels. He certainly wasn't going to fall
head over heels in love with her and settle down in
Roseville—or Fort Wayne for that matter. Campbell
Industries would someday soon be his responsibility. He would be coming back from Philadelphia this
time, but in a few weeks his work in Roseville would
be finished and she would be lucky if she saw him
two or three times a year. That was reality.

She caught herself thinking about the banks in
Philadelphia, then dismissed the idea. Sure, he'd
said he would take her with him when he left, but
she wasn't naïve. Men often said such things in the
heat of passion. No, the facts were clear. She was in
love with a man who would only be around for a
few weeks at best.

The telephone rang and she jumped at the shrill
sound. The second insistent ring brought her out of
the tub. Wrapping a fluffy bath towel around her
dripping body, Carla hurried into her bedroom.

"Yes," she managed, trying to keep the towel up
with one hand, the telephone in place with the other.

"How's my favorite feminist doing tonight?" Trent
asked, his voice low and seductive.

"Dripping," she laughed, unable to suppress her
joy at hearing his voice. "You got me out of a bath."

"Want to turn this into an obscene phone call?
You can tell me what you're wearing and I'll pant a
lot."

"Feminists abhor obscene phone calls," Carla returned as solemnly as possible. She hadn't giggled

since she was a teenager, but she felt dangerously close to doing so now.

"Lady, you're cruel. Just one suggestive remark?"

"Trent Campbell, you're crazy. You called me long distance for this?"

"I called you long distance because I missed the sound of your voice. In fact, I miss *all* of you." His tone was blatantly suggestive.

She laughed. "How was your flight?"

"Uneventful. Samples are now in the labs, hopefully to be tested tomorrow. Had dinner with my father. He agrees that Roseville sounds like a good location. What did you have for dinner?"

His question caught her off guard. "A spinach soufflé. Why?"

"You made a soufflé?" He sounded surprised.

"No." She giggled, collapsing on the bed and rolling over on her back. "Every soufflé I've tried absolutely refused to rise. This one was store bought."

"How can I fall asleep envisioning you slaving away over a hot stove, if you keep telling me you're a lousy cook? What were you going to fix if I'd come to dinner tonight?"

"Steaks, they're my standby for company. But sometimes I even burn them."

It was Trent's turn to laugh. "The decision's been made. We leave the finances to you and the cooking to me."

They talked a while longer—laughing and joking. The click of the receiver, when he did hang up, seemed cold and distant. But Carla was happy. Trent had called and soon he would be back. It wasn't until the next day at the bank, that she cursed him for ever leaving.

"CAN WE TALK TO YOU?" asked Karen Pierce, shyly tapping on Carla's door.

Karen was Ken Pierce's wife and with her were Bob Dolman's wife, Sue, and Neil Higgins's wife, Alice.

"We know you're seeing a lot of that man connected with the chemical plant," Karen continued, "and we hoped you could help us."

"Come on in," motioned Carla, putting down her pen and rising to her feet. The reference to Trent made her pulse rush a little faster than normal, but she tried to appear calm and efficient as the three women entered her office. "What can I do for you?"

"It's the chemicals, our water—" Karen began.

"I don't want two thousand people invading our town," interrupted Alice.

"Where would they all live?" groaned Sue.

Carla tried to answer the women, but discovered it was impossible. Each wanted a say.

"Can you imagine two thousand houses? Our farmland would be ruined."

"Our little town would disappear. Why, in no time we'd be a suburb of Fort Wayne—nothing more."

"Think of the advantages," Carla inserted. "Better schools, better—"

"I like small schools where I know the teachers and my children's friends," argued Sue. "Lord knows what kind of people would move here."

"Well-educated people for the most part," Carla attempted to explain. "And they wouldn't all live in Roseville. Many would commute from Fort Wayne."

"Worse yet," muttered Alice, "traffic would become a problem."

"It would mean better roads—"

"Higher taxes."

"Baker Labs would help your tax situation."

"Crime would increase," moaned Karen. "I can walk the streets alone at night and not worry. I know everyone around here and everyone knows me. I'm in no danger. There's a feeling of trust and security in Roseville. But if that many people moved here, everything would change."

"Ladies, ladies," Carla finally cried in exasperation. "Let's discuss this one point at a time."

She did manage to establish some semblance of order, but by the time the three women left her office, Carla's head was reeling, and she walked out into the lobby for a break. Problems she'd never envisioned had been voiced. Real concerns to the residents of Roseville.

"Have you heard about the chemical plant?" Carla asked Hazel, needing to use the head teller as a sounding board.

"The whole town has. Felix Gordon put out a special edition of the paper this morning. The entire issue is devoted to that Campbell fellow and his chemical plant. I imagine you'll have a lot of people poppin' in to talk to you today."

"Why me?" Carla was already dreading the thought.

The older woman seemed surprised that she even had to ask. "Everyone knows you and he have been seein' a lot of each other lately."

"I've been acting as his guide, showing Mr. Campbell around the area," Carla said, hoping to protect her image.

"Seth Harcort said he saw you two actin' *real*

friendly Saturday afternoon." Hazel's brown eyes twinkled and Carla blushed. So much for the image.

"I'll be in my office," she mumbled, deciding to forget the discussion she'd planned on having with Hazel.

She accomplished little work that day or the next. People were stopping by every few minutes. Some had positive comments, stating the town needed an industry like Baker Labs to keep it alive. But for the most part Carla listened to concerns. Environmental pollution, to her surprise, was not the primary worry. It was the quality of life that most people didn't want changed.

Customers she had never personally met before came to her door to voice their opinions. Gordon's article had stirred up everyone for miles around the town and her name had been romantically linked with Trent's. With him gone, she became the logical one to speak to.

"How goes it?" Trent asked when he called Wednesday night.

"Not well. I've spent all day talking to people about Baker Labs," she soberly relayed. "Wood's going to be on my tail if I don't get my bank reports done soon."

"That bad?"

"I don't know, Trent." She sighed, feeling the burden of listening to so many points of view beginning to tell. "Oh sure, I knew there'd be some resistance to the idea, but I never expected this much."

"Don't worry. I think I can convince everyone there's no danger of pollution. We run a clean plant. Our past record is our best defense."

"It's not just pollution. I wish you were here,

Trent. I wish you could see and listen to these people." It was impossible to translate worried facial expressions into words.

"I'll be there soon, honey. I'm sorry all of this fell on you. Those lab reports are taking longer than I expected and dad's had me in his office every day. I know he'd like to hand it all over to me. I just wish he'd wait a little while longer."

THURSDAY CARLA HAD TO CLOSE her door and ignore the knocks. The bank report came first. Wood wouldn't wait. But once her door was opened, the stream of people began again. By closing time Carla was exhausted.

"Do feminists accept rides?" a deep, familiar voice called out as she walked home from the bank.

"Trent!" she cried, turning to see his beige Cadillac pull up beside her.

"Hop in, I want to show you something." Leaning across the seat, Trent pushed open her door.

"When did you get back?" she asked, slipping in beside him and smoothing the flared skirt of her teal-blue shirtdress.

"This afternoon. You look lovely, Miss Parker. If I didn't know how you felt about public shows of affections, I'd grab you and kiss you."

"And if Neil Higgins wasn't watching from his station, I might let you." She grinned and reached across the console to take his hand. "You're looking good, Mr. Campbell."

A powder-blue polo shirt replaced his usual dress shirt, tie and jacket. His slate-gray slacks were crisp and neatly pressed, hugging his hips and delineating the sinewy muscles of his thighs. He'd been gone three days and it seemed an eternity. She longed to be in his arms, feel his lips on hers.

"Only two blocks and you're all mine." He sighed, his fingers tightening around hers.

"Two blocks to where?" Her house was only one block away.

"Emma Gordon's house," he explained. "I took your advice and talked to Felix Gordon about a place to stay while I was in town. He suggested his mother's. Seems she's in California for the summer." Trent pulled up in front of an old two-story brick house, with a small wooden porch and white shutters on the windows.

"Did you read the special edition Felix put out about Baker Labs?" Carla asked, opening her own door and meeting Trent on the sidewalk.

"I did, and as far as I'm concerned, he presented a fair, unbiased summary of my plans."

"It certainly stirred up the people around town."

Trent opened the front door and they stepped into a cool, dark foyer. "Alone, at last," he said, pulling her to him as the door clicked shut. "Now, what was that you said about letting me kiss you?"

"I said, I might let you." She grinned mischievously.

"No might about it." He took her mouth hungrily, tasting her, possessing her. His large hand pressed against the small of her back, molding her to him and she offered no resistance.

For three long, restless nights, ever since she'd accepted the fact that she did love him, she'd dreamed of being held like this, of giving herself to him completely. Her arms wrapped around his neck, her fingers combing through his hair, mussing it, then smoothing it back into place. He kissed her as though he feared she might disappear. His lips bruised hers. His hands roamed freely over her body.

"I wanted to come back yesterday. But one report—one stupid test—kept me away."

"I was so glad you called last night." Her response was breathless. He might not love her as she did him, but he needed her and for the moment that was enough. His fingers slid over her breasts and she groaned.

"This is better than a telephone call, any day." His mouth once again captured hers and she could taste his desire. Every stroke of his hand, every thrust of his tongue told her of his need for her. And she willingly responded, no longer afraid.

When he lifted his head, she stared at him, memorizing every wonderful line of his face. His eyes were dark. Darker than she remembered. *Bedroom eyes.* The term was one her mother always used to describe certain movie actors. It seemed appropriate now. Carla knew where they were headed. The time had come.

Then Trent swore. "Dammit, Carla, every time I get my hands on you, I forget all my good intentions. I brought you here to fix you a home-cooked meal, not to seduce you."

Immediately, he let go of her. Dazed, Carla took his hand when he offered it and followed him, not to the bedroom, but to Emma Gordon's kitchen.

"I've got a special meal planned for tonight," he said, opening the refrigerator. "I hope you're hungry."

Hungry? She was starved, but not for food. Her

legs were shaking, her entire body begging for his touch. "You're going to cook dinner?" she mumbled.

"Miss Parker," he grinned, looking back over his shoulder as he handed her a chilly, cellophane bag, "I am going to prove to you that it's easy to prepare a home-cooked meal, that even a dyed-in-the-wool feminist could fix one." Next came two lemons.

Carla set each of the items he handed her on the counter. It seemed he was determined to feed her. "You know, if I help, something's bound to go wrong."

"Then just watch. Keep me company. Tell me all of the local gossip." He rinsed off two plump chicken breasts and patted them dry.

"*We're* the hottest item of gossip. Seth Harcort's been telling everyone that he saw us kissing out by the lake."

Trent paused in his preparations, ignoring the butter sizzling in the frying pan. "I'm sorry, Carla. I never thought he'd come to shore that early or I wouldn't have—"

She shrugged her shoulders. "I wasn't exactly an innocent bystander, you know. Do you want this broccoli rinsed?"

"Yes, please." He frowned as he watched her move to the sink. "What's being said about us?"

Carla grinned, more to herself than to Trent. "That we're 'keeping company.' Those are Miss Atherby's words. She asked about you. Wanted to know where that nice young man I was keeping company with was."

Trent chuckled. "She's sweet. Reminds me of my grandmother."

"What do I do next?" Carla shook the head of broccoli, then set it into a colander to drain.

"Find some wineglasses and while I get dinner ready we can have some of the Riesling I bought."

Jelly glasses were the best Carla could come up with, and Trent laughed as they clinked the rims of the solidly made glasses together. "How can I seduce you with wine served in jelly glasses?"

"You can try," she teased.

Trent studied her for a moment, then smiled and returned to the stove where the chicken breasts were cooking.

His rice was fluffy, the broccoli *al dente*—its rich green color enhancing Emma Gordon's inexpensive china—and Carla would have sworn the lemon sauce Trent prepared for the chicken was better than anything she'd ever tasted. "You learned all of this from your uncle?" she asked.

"No, Uncle Clay simply got me interested in cooking. A few years ago I took a class in gourmet cooking. I enjoy it. It's one way for me to relax."

"Just the opposite for me. Whenever I cook, I end up frustrated. Something always goes wrong. My rice never comes out like this. Even when I use the brand that's guaranteed to be a success, I fail."

He chuckled. "What you need is a maid."

"No!" Carla's eyes clouded, her thoughts reverting to her childhood, to the years she watched her mother serve her father. No woman would ever have to serve her.

"I forgot. Job stereotyping, right? How about a houseboy then, or whatever they call the male counterpart of a maid?"

He was trying to make her smile, and she did.

There was no way he could know his innocent comment had hit a raw nerve ending, that her reaction was due to her mother's and father's relationship, not to a feminist viewpoint. "Houseboy," she laughed. "Now that would be a unique situation in Roseville."

"How are you doing as my go-between?" he finally asked. "Any new objections to Baker Labs?"

"Mostly what I've told you over the telephone. The town is dividing into two groups—those who want the plant here and those who don't. I don't know, Trent. I've heard some say they're going to oppose your petition to change the zoning of the Clayton farm from agricultural to commercial."

"There will probably be a hearing, then. Will you put in a good word for me?"

"Of course. In fact, I've been ordered to. Thorton Wood called me just this morning. I sent him a copy of Felix Gordon's special edition of the paper. I was clearly told to offer you any and all assistance you might need."

Wood's attitude had irritated her, although she'd been careful not to let him know that. It seemed as though he didn't trust her ability to carry out this matter of simple diplomacy. She hadn't told him she was seeing Trent socially. She already knew her boss didn't approve of mixing business with pleasure.

After dinner Trent and Carla put away the leftover food and cleaned the kitchen. He'd made decaffeinated coffee, and when they were finished with the dishes they took their steaming mugs of the brew into the living room, where they sat on the faded crushed-velvet sofa.

As Trent sipped his coffee, Carla studied his face.

A shadow of beard darkened his chin. In the past few nights she had often pictured him like this, remembered the way he would quirk one eyebrow when he was angry or amused. If anyone had ever told her she would fall in love with a man in just a few days, she would have told him he was crazy. That was, up to a week ago she would have. Now she knew she was the crazy one.

The sun was setting outside, its rosy glow penetrating the closed draperies. The rain had ended two days before, the last of the clouds were now mere wisps, and the sky was ablaze with color. The living room took on a radiance that was reflected in Carla's iridescent eyes. Trent noticed it and set down his mug. Reaching over, he touched her cheek.

Carla sat immobile, caught by the magic of the moment. Her breathing became shallow, barely noticeable. Her heart seeming to stop. His fingertips traced the curve of her lips, then the line of her jaw. Oh, how she loved him.

Like a sorcerer weaving his spell Trent trailed his fingers along the contours of her face, pushing back a strand of hair, moving over her fine eyebrows, down the straight line of her nose. Again he touched her lips.

They were drawing together, pulled by some unknown force. He took her mug from her hand and set it beside his. Carla waited, afraid to speak, afraid words might tell him the love she felt for him. Her eyes closed when his mouth grazed hers, her hands reaching up to feel his shoulders.

He murmured her name over and over, each kiss growing more demanding, each caress more erotic. The pins were removed and her hair fell to her shoulders. Her movements blended naturally with his, as waves of craving swept over her. He stroked, nuzzled and nibbled, and each flick of his tongue set her pulse racing faster.

Somehow her dress was removed, along with his shirt. Then her bra fell by the couch and springy, tight curls pressed against warm, soft breasts. Every breath was a pleasure, bringing the scent of him, forcing her velvety smooth skin against the hardness of his chest.

"I'm going to make love to you," he murmured, then paused, waiting for her refusal. But there was none.

The room was dark when he lifted her from the couch and carried her to the bedroom. A quick tug and the covers were yanked back, only the springs of the old bed voicing a faint protest when Trent placed her on the soft cotton sheet. Again the bed groaned when Trent settled himself beside her.

Carla stared at him, his shadowy form barely visible, no more than a dark silhouette against a background of white. Her stomach tightened with anxiety.

"Tonight will be special," he breathed against her cheek, as if reading her thoughts. "I promise."

Slowly, expertly he turned her hesitancy into anticipation. His softly sucking mouth played over hers, enticing her to respond. Gently he touched her breasts, his fingertips sliding possessively over each, catching a nipple between his forefinger and thumb and sending currents of excitement throughout her. And when his lips followed the path of his hands, she moaned in elemental pleasure, forgetting everything but the throbbing, growing desire he was arousing.

His hand moved over her silky petticoat, small, circular strokes investigating the flat lines of her stomach, the rounded curve of her bottom and the length of her thigh. Willingly Carla opened herself to his exploration. She needed him.

"Undress me," Trent whispered in the darkness.

Carla hesitated only a moment. Trembling fingers found his belt buckle and loosened it. As she fumbled with the zipper, he cupped her face in his hands, lovingly kissing her. "I need you so much," he rasped, then groaned as her fingertips brushed against his hard male outline.

"I'm not very good at this," Carla apologized, her voice quavering.

"You're doing fine."

He helped her, shedding his clothes in one easy movement. Taking her hands, he guided them over his body, patiently waiting until she was at ease with their differences, groaning as she touched him in the special places that gave him pleasure. Then he turned his attention to her.

There was no awkwardness as he expertly removed her undergarments, dropping them over the edge of the bed before trailing kisses from her breasts to the mound of reddish hairs, every touch of his lips setting her afire. Then his mouth moved lower.

"Trent...no," she gasped. Never had a man kissed her there.

"I want to know all of you," he responded, his fingers beginning to explore the forbidden area.

Embarrassment turned to curiosity, then need. A gripping, consuming ache twisted through her. Her legs parted, inviting him to continue his investigation and, as his mouth found the treasure he sought, her fingers combed into his thick, vibrant hair, her breathing coming in short, spasmodic gasps.

It was ecstasy; it was pain. A flurry of sensations washed over her. *More.* She wanted more of him— all of him. "Trent, please—" she cried as his tongue flicked out to further ignite her.

"Yes, my love, yes," he promised, leaving her moist, feminine mound and moving up her body.

Writhing beneath him, Carla moaned. Never before had she known such a consuming need. Her fingers dug into his back and she groaned. A primeval force had taken command, instinct guiding her actions as she moved against him, enticing, offering.

"Easy, honey, easy," he murmured, tempering her movements. "This isn't the best time to ask, but is it safe? Do I need to use something?"

It took a second before Carla realized what he was talking about. Her voice was husky, the words coming spasmodically. "Tuesday...I renewed my prescription...it's all right...it's safe."

Her assurance was the catalyst Trent needed. Opposites became one—hard molding to soft, male to female. At first his thrusts were slow and deep, each bringing her greater pleasure than the last, then he picked up his tempo, his quick pulsing rhythm carrying her to the edge of bliss. Her fingers tightened on his shoulders, her hips arching beneath his exquisite weight. She was close—so very close.

But his need was too great, his abstinence too long. Trent moved beyond her, his breathing coming in short, fitful gasps, his body shuddering. He cried out her name and Carla knew he'd crossed that fine line without her.

7

"THAT WASN'T THE WAY I'd planned it," Trent apologized, his body moist with perspiration as he held her close.

"That's all right," Carla murmured.

"It's been so long since I've been with anyone. I'm afraid I just couldn't wait for you."

"Forget it."

"I'll make it up to you," Trent promised, trying to kiss her, but missing her mouth in the dark.

"I should be getting home." Carla bit her lower lip. Wiggling, she discovered that Trent had her pinned to the mattress with one arm.

"Spend the night with me." He found her ear, his tongue darting in and out in a suggestive manner.

"I can't. Trent, stop that!"

"Why can't you?"

"I can't be seen coming out of your house in the morning. Keeping company is one thing. Having an affair is quite another. Don't forget, I am manager of the bank." She tried again to escape his hold, only to find herself pinioned to the mattress, Trent arched over her.

"All right, I'll get you home at a decent hour, but before you go we have some unfinished business."

"What business?" Her voice seemed to be caught in her throat, the words barely more than a whisper.

As he pressed his hips against hers, her eyes widened. He was fully aroused. "But I thought...I mean...you just...."

"You've heard of rapid growth and rising interest, haven't you?" He captured her bottom with his warm hands, pulling her to him. "Besides, we have *your* account to consider."

"Trent," she groaned as a new, unfamiliar sensation curled in the pit of her stomach. His thighs were hard as iron as they pushed against her legs. Leaning back, he lifted her hips, fusing them as one.

It was a new experience for Carla, having her needs focused upon. Trent made love to her with words, as well as with his body. There was no rush to his movements. His fingertips slid over the hardened peaks of her breasts, along the curves of her body to the sensitive cradle of her femininity. Slowly, surely he caressed her, one sensation building on the next until she was like a finely tuned instrument, keyed to the slightest touch.

And then that moment came, when he struck that perfect chord and she could wait no longer. Convulsing, shuddering, she cried out, mindless of her words, totally oblivious to all else but the rhythms of her body.

And he followed, leaning over her, thrusting deeper and deeper and repeating her name, until he was taken over by a series of tremors.

Carla didn't move as Trent rolled to her side. Staring at the ceiling, her breathing still ragged, she was silent as he ran his fingertips over her warm, damp skin. Never before had she felt such an overpowering need or such a complete release. Frustration had turned to satisfaction. For the first time in her life she felt totally a woman, and the feeling was good.

"You all right?" he asked softly, brushing her hair back from where it clung to the sides of her face.

"I never realized it could be like that," she said, turning and trying to discern his features in the darkness.

"You and Dan?" He left the question up to her.

"Yes, but nothing like what you and I just shared. Believe it or not, that was a first for me."

"I'm glad." Trent cradled her close. "I felt so badly before. It was so frustrating, not being able to wait for you."

"You think you were frustrated." It seemed good to be able to laugh about it.

He also laughed. "Honey, I've been frustrated ever since I met you. I've taken so many cold showers this past week, it's amazing I haven't caught pneumonia."

"I imagine you're used to getting your way with women." She knew few would have resisted as long as she had.

"Hey." He cuddled her close, gently nipping her ear with his teeth. "Knowing a woman is available, and wanting her are two different things. I'm a very selective man, Carla Jayne."

"And I'm a very selective woman." She kissed him on the tip of his nose, then sighed and lay back on the bed. "I suppose I should be getting home."

"Not yet," he murmured, his hand lazily caressing the contours of her breasts. "Stay a while longer."

"If I stay much longer, I'm liable to fall asleep." Already her lids felt heavy. Still, it would be nice to lie here just a little longer, nestled against his warmth. "What time is it?" she mumbled.

Trent pushed the button on his watch, lighting the figures. "A little past eleven."

"That late?" Immediately alert, Carla sat up, swinging her feet over the edge of the bed. In the dark she began to grope for her underwear.

The light by the bed came on, its brightness catching her off guard. She turned to see Trent, his hand still on the switch, his body stretched out across the bed. He looked like a Greek statue, his muscles beautifully defined and taut, his manhood relaxed. He smiled and sat up. "Take a shower before you leave. It will make you feel better. Then I'll walk you home and you can go straight to bed."

"I don't know."

He gave her little choice. Sliding off the bed, Trent took her hand and led her to a small bathroom. There he turned on the faucets, until a warm, steamy mist filled the room. "I suppose I would feel better," she admitted and shoved her hair into the flowered shower cap he handed her.

"Guaranteed to eliminate morning-after aches and pains."

Carla slipped behind the shower curtain and sighed as the hot, invigorating spray washed over her skin. Then she gasped as the curtain moved and Trent stepped in beside her. "What are you doing?"

"Taking some of my own advice." Picking up the bar of soap, he made a lather, then began to efficiently spread it over his entire body.

"If you don't mind, I generally take my showers alone." There was barely room for the two of them in the cramped space.

"I certainly hope so." Leaning close, he planted a kiss on her forehead, the lather from his body transferring to hers. 'Step aside, lady, I need to rinse off."

"You're insufferable," she grumbled, inching her
way past him. A tingling sensation spiraled through
her as her breasts brushed against his chest and his
hips touched hers.

"I can't help it if it takes you women all day to
bathe," he teased, then handed her the bar of soap
and stepped out of the shower stall.

Carla took her time washing. She wasn't quite certain how to deal with the ache growing deep inside
of her. She'd always believed she had a low sex
drive; yet being so close to Trent, seeing him naked,
had touched off a yearning she could barely control.

When she stepped from the shower, he was standing in front of a steamy mirror, toweling his hair dry.
Although she'd purposely dallied, he still hadn't
dressed. The ache flamed into desire.

He had a magnificent physique and she longed to
reach out and slide her fingers down his back. She
remembered a calendar of men's derrières. Trent's
would have been a good one to include.

He turned and caught her staring at his bottom
and Carla was glad her skin was already flushed
from the heat of the shower. She knew she was
blushing.

"You know, Miss Parker, you have a very beautiful body."

"I was just thinking the same about you."

He smiled, grabbed a towel from the rack and
stepped toward her. The shower cap was pulled
from her head, her hair cascading to her shoulders.
Then gently, thoroughly, he dried her, the towel becoming a sensuous extension of his hands.

Carla moaned as he pulled her close, her breasts pressing against his chest, the towel being slowly drawn down her back, welding them together. "I want you again," he groaned. "I can't seem to get enough of you." His mouth covered hers and the line of contact was completed.

Carla responded to his kiss by wrapping her arms around his neck and arching her back. Someday he would be gone and this night would be no more than a memory. She would have other nights, lonely nights, when she would catch up on her sleep. Tonight she wanted to be loved.

He carried her into the bedroom and lay her across the bed. The brilliance of the light gave their lovemaking a new dimension. He touched, he kissed and when she asked, he showed her ways she could please him. There were no secrets; no taboos. She loved him, loved the way he made her feel. And when she could no longer think straight, she closed her eyes and surrendered to the savage sweetness of his possession. Writhing, trembling, she gave to him as honestly as he gave himself to her.

"Now we need another shower," Trent chuckled as they lay together, their bodies damp with perspiration.

"This could go on all night," Carla purred.

It was nearly three when Trent walked her up the steps of her porch. Only the moon and the streetlight illuminated them as Trent kissed her. Feeling like a teenager sneaking in past curfew, Carla glanced furtively across the street and was relieved to see Miss Atherby's lights were out. "See you tomorrow," Trent whispered, then left.

FRIDAY MORNING THE ALARM seemed unusually loud and insistent, but by the time she arrived at the bank, C.J. Parker looked every bit the efficient manager she was. Only the sparkle in her hazel eyes and the quickness of her smile hinted at the joy in her heart.

Trent called just before noon. She'd half expected, half hoped he would stop by and take her out to lunch, and the sound of his voice on the telepone left her disappointed. "I'm in Fort Wayne checking out the deed on the Clayton farm," he explained. "I'm going to be tied up most of the day. Are you free tonight?"

"Hmm, let me check my calendar," she teased. "Ah, yes.... I do have an opening tonight."

"You'd better. We're going to dinner at your boss's house."

"Thorton Wood's?" she said in surprise. "How did you get an invitation to his place?"

"He called me this morning. Seems he's been trying to get hold of me ever since you sent him that article, but it took him until today to track me down. My secretary must have given him my Roseville number within minutes after I called and gave it to her."

"What did he want?" It was strange that Wood had called Trent, especially since Trent wasn't really a bank client—yet.

"To talk. Since I'm going to be busy all day, he suggested dinner at his place. I told him I'd planned on spending the evening with the loveliest woman in Indiana, and he said to bring her along. So, I'm asking... will you go with me?"

"But you didn't specifically tell him you were bringing me?"

"No—why? Should I have?" Trent sounded confused.

Carla hesitated, trying to think of the best way to explain the situation. "Thorton Wood doesn't make a practice of fraternizing with his employees. He might not welcome my presence tonight."

"Nonsense! What man in his right mind wouldn't welcome a beautiful, intelligent woman into his house?"

She could hear the warmth in Trent's voice and her desire to be with him overrode any qualms she had about her boss's reaction.

"Would you like me to call him?" asked Trent, not entirely oblivious to her concern.

"No, that's all right." There was no sense in putting Wood in an awkward position. She would call him herself. "I'd love to go with you."

"Good. I miss you. My bed seemed awfully lonely this morning."

Carla lowered her voice, even though her door was closed. "Trent, what if someone should hear you?"

"Who's going to hear me? No one here knows whom I'm talking to." He laughed. "Are you blushing, my love?"

"Of course not." But her cheeks were flushed and she had to chuckle. "Is this another one of your obscene phone calls?"

"Nope. I'm just disappointed. I would much rather be having lunch with you than staring at page after page of legal documents. Sleep well last night?"

"Like a log. What little sleep I did get. How about you?"

"Fantastic. Amazing what eliminating a little frustration will do for one."

They talked for a while, neither wanting to hang up, until a knock at Carla's door disturbed them. "I'll pick you up at six," he told her before saying goodbye.

SHE DID TRY to call Wood. Several times she rang his office only to be informed by his secretary that he was out, but she would be certain he called the Roseville branch as soon as he returned. Her call still hadn't been returned by the time Carla left her office but she hesitated calling him at his home. She would simply have to hope Wood understood the situation.

When Trent rang the doorbell, she was ready, her hair arranged so that one side was swept back behind her ear, the other curling softly over her shoulder. Her nail polish was a soft peach, to match the gossamer flower print on the sheer crepe she'd chosen to wear, while her mascara brought out the green of her eyes. Everything about her was light and airy, the shirred shoulders of the dress exposing her long, graceful arms, the spaghetti belt accentuating her small waist. It was the most feminine dress she owned and she felt sexy and alluring as she walked down the stairs, the skirt swirling softly around her knees.

Her white high-heeled sandals were open at the toes and she'd taken the time to paint her toenails, the color now muted beneath the hazy weave of her pantyhose. Long, lacy filigree chains of gold hung from her earlobes, the precious metal glinting whenever she shook her head. One caught the light of the sun when she opened the door and looked up into Trent's eyes.

"Beautiful," he murmured, staring at her. A smile curved his lips as he reached out to touch the ends of the golden chains, his head tilting closer until his mouth found hers.

"Miss Atherby," Carla reminded him and he stepped farther into the house and pushed the door closed.

"Forget Miss Atherby. I've waited all day for this." He sighed, his lips playing across hers, his tongue tasting her lipstick.

Carla wrapped her arms around him, letting him draw her closer. He smelled good, the familiar, manly scent of his body blending with a musky cologne. And beneath her fingers the fine gabardine of his slate-gray suit felt smooth and cool.

"Trent," she groaned and shivered as he nuzzled her hair and nipped at her shoulder. "Dinner?"

"You taste delicious," he murmured, then looked up and grinned. "I suppose you're right. We should get going before I get totally distracted."

"How do you manage to keep all of your diverse companies running smoothly, if you're so easily distracted?" she teased as he held the car door open for her.

"Believe it or not, I usually don't have any trouble. I guess I just have a weakness for feminists with reddish-brown hair and eyes that change color with every mood." He brushed her lips with a kiss as she slid past him, then walked around to the driver's side.

"I've only been to Wood's house once," Carla told

Trent as they drove out of town. "It was a cocktail party for all of the new bank officers. Beautiful place."

That had been a pleasant evening, if somewhat formal. What Wood's reaction would be when he saw her at his door tonight, she didn't know. Her dress, her hairdo—even her makeup—were far more feminine than anything she'd ever worn to a business affair. But earlier, as she'd dressed, she hadn't been thinking about her boss. Trent was the one she'd wanted to impress...and his response had been worth the time and effort. Now, as they neared Fort Wayne, she hoped she hadn't been too impulsive.

Thorton Wood's home was north of the city in a semi-wooded setting. Well back from the road, the two-story white house with its shuttered, lead-paned windows, looked as expensive as Carla was certain it was. The lawn on either side of the curving sidewalk was lush and well manicured and the shrubbery around the house added rich touches of green.

Trent rang the doorbell, then turned to face her. In his designer suit he looked the proper businessman. His tweed silk tie—a gold tie pin holding it in place—matched the maroon pocket square in his breast pocket. The cuff of his pin-striped silk shirt brushed against her cheek as he reached up to push an errant strand of hair back behind her ear.

When Thorton Wood answered the door, he seemed a bit taken aback, but quickly recovered. "Why, Carla, how nice."

"I tried to call you at your office and let you know I was coming," she explained, hoping he would understand she hadn't meant to intrude upon his hospitality.

"Ah, yes, I did see a message to call you. I'm afraid I'd been out on a real estate deal all day and put off all of my calls until tomorrow." Turning to Trent, he offered his hand. "Mr. Campbell. So glad you could make it tonight."

"My pleasure. And please, call me Trent," Trent insisted, shaking the bank president's hand.

"And you must call me Thorton."

As they stood in the doorway, dispensing with the amenities, Carla studied her employer. Thorton Wood was a dignified looking man. His hair was thinning and a bald spot at the back was no longer completely covered by the neatly cut brown hairs, but the gray at his sideburns added a distinguished touch. Carla had never seen him in anything but neutral colored clothing and the midnight blue chalk-striped suit he was wearing this evening was no exception.

Thorton Wood's chest had slipped some, his midriff showing the effect of too many desserts and his sixty-one years, but Carla knew he played golf at least twice a week and handball once in a while. In all, his physique was that of a much younger man.

His eyes were brown, although not the rich, velvety shade of Trent's, and his tanned face had a healthy glow. The one thing that had always left her feeling ill at ease around her boss was his short stature. Even in flats she had to look down at him and she sensed that that bothered him. Tonight she towered above him.

"We're having cocktails before dinner, out by the pool," Thorton stated. "Follow me."

He led the way past an elegant, curved staircase, down two steps to the formal living room. An L-shaped Lawson sofa and Queen Anne wing chair were upholstered in off-white, the same shade as the sculptured area rug. The muted colors brought out the detail in the Georgian Court tables, Duncan Phyfe arm chair and imported accents. It was a handsome room. Carla remembered admiring it the first time she'd been in the house. French doors opened onto a patio and as Carla stepped through them, she saw Dan.

He was seated beside Mary Anne, on a white wrought-iron love seat. His back was turned to her, but she recognized him immediately and paused. "You all right?" Trent asked softly.

"Fine, just surprised that he's here," she murmured so that no one else could hear.

"What would you two like to drink?" asked Thorton, going behind a wet bar.

It was then Dan turned to face them and saw her. Carla smiled, took Trent's arm and walked on to the bar. Dan's shocked expression made his being there worthwhile.

"Carla we never expected *you*," was Mary Anne's blunt greeting.

"I'd like a gin and tonic," answered Carla, responding to Thorton Wood's question. There was no graceful answer to Mary Anne's comment.

"Why, Miss Parker, what a pleasant surprise," said Velma Wood, Thorton's gracious, if somewhat flighty wife, as she came out onto the patio from the kitchen. "I was just talking to the maid and didn't hear you arrive. Dinner will be ready in a few minutes." Her floor-length blue hostess gown skimmed the gray slate stones as she approached the bar.

Thorton introduced his wife to Trent, then proceeded to mix the drinks. "You must see my roses," Velma said, as soon as her husband handed Carla her gin and tonic. "I'm so proud of them this year. Come along, Mary Anne. Keep us company."

Carla wasn't certain if it was a planned maneuver or chance, but Velma insisted Carla and Mary Anne join her, leaving Thorton, Trent and Dan to talk. The idea of staying and listening to what the men had to say—especially about Baker Labs—was far more appealing to her than looking at roses, but she knew it would be impolite to refuse, so Carla followed her boss's wife into the garden.

Velma rambled on and on about this and that particular variety of rose and the battle she'd been waging against the aphids. Carla could have cared less, and longed to rejoin the men. Mary Anne also seemed totally uninterested in her mother's plight and watched Carla closely. "I do hope it doesn't bother you, my being with Dan tonight," Mary Anne commented when Carla and she were momentarily alone.

"No problem." Carla pretended to admire a yellow rosebud.

"He told me you were quite upset when he broke off your engagement."

"When *he* broke the engagement?" Carla's eyebrows automatically rose. It would be typical of Dan to twist matters around to suit himself. Mary Anne nodded.

"Things aren't always as they appear," Carla said diplomatically.

"But Dan—" Carla knew Mary Anne would have liked to talk more about Dan, that something was bothering her, but her mother came back just then to see what was keeping them, and Mary Anne said no more.

It seemed an eternity before their tour of the garden was complete and they returned to the patio. Trent looked over and smiled, and Carla stepped to his side.

"We were discussing the potential growth for the Roseville bank if Trent's company should move there," Thorton stated, closely regarding Carla as Trent casually slipped his arm around her waist. "I hope you realize what a bonus this will be for you."

"Then you won't be closing the Roseville branch?" Carla asked, certain she already knew the answer.

"No...of course not." He was obviously flustered and glanced at Trent, to assure himself that Trent hadn't been disturbed by Carla's comment. "Where did you hear that?"

"Just last week Mary Anne mentioned that you'd been discussing the possibility with Dan."

"Just talk," Thorton returned, glaring at his daughter. Then he looked at Trent. "You know, speculation...what if?"

"It was *not* just talk," Mary Anne spoke up, indignant over her father's silent rebuke. "I clearly recall the discussion. It was the night Dan took me to the movies. He showed you that report with the statistics on how many people had moved out of Roseville in the last ten years, and you said yourself that it wouldn't be profitable to keep the Roseville branch open much longer."

So it *was* Dan who had started Wood thinking

about closing the Roseville branch. Was he still afraid of her?

Neither Dan nor Wood seemed pleased by Mary Anne's reminder of their conversation. "Statistics can be misleading," Thorton hurried to assure Trent. "Roseville's a fine, growing community."

"Exactly what Carla told me," answered Trent, tightening his hold around her waist.

Dan paled and Carla was certain he remembered the caustic remarks he'd made about Roseville when they'd met in the hotel restaurant. His discomfort amused her.

"Dinner is served," called a young woman from an open door.

They all followed Velma into a long, stately dining room filled with solid-oak furnishings and high-backed chairs. No particular period dominated the decor of the house, but quality and cost were evident everywhere Carla looked. She was seated on Trent's right, next to Thorton and across from Mary Anne. Dan faced Trent, Velma at the opposite end of the table between the two men. As everyone seated themselves, Carla lifted a delicately patterned blue wineglass and studied it.

"It looks as though you and Velma share a love of depression glass," murmured Trent, watching her.

"Except her pocket book is plumper than mine. These are *Versailles* blues. They represent Depression Era glassware, rather than depression glass, per se. Even in the thirties these glasses sold in the finer department stores. Today this wine goblet alone would probably go for forty to fifty dollars."

Trent studied the glass closer.

"Have you opened an account at our Roseville office?'' asked Wood, noting the relaxed manner Carla had around Trent. It was impossible for him to miss the shared glances or ignore how radiant Carla looked. Even Dan was watching her closely, virtually ignoring Mary Anne.

''Not yet,'' answered Trent, setting down the glass. ''I don't believe in putting the cart before the horse, to borrow a phrase. I still have a lot of work to do before the final okay is given to move Baker Labs to Roseville.''

''Such as what?'' asked Dan, his golden eyebrows puckering slightly as his gaze left Carla to focus on Trent.

''Such as drainage reports, several environmental studies and a zoning change. I find it best to be thorough. The results usually pay off.'' Trent's hand touched Carla's and she twined her fingers through his.

The gesture seemed to disturb Dan, but not Wood. ''I see my manager isn't going to let you slip through her fingers until she does have you signed,'' Thorton grinned. ''I've always said a woman can do more with a smile than a man can do in hours of negotiations.''

''I don't think a smile or any talk from me would sway Trent,'' Carla responded quickly. ''As he said, his decision will be determined by outside factors. And right now Roseville is divided on the issue of Baker Labs. The township might not allow the plant to locate there.''

''Those fools,'' blurted Wood, hitting the table with his fist so the glassware rattled. ''I swear those people are living in the past.''

''They have a reason to be concerned,'' Carla defended, pulling her hand free from Trent's. "If Baker Labs comes to Roseville, the town will change. It will never again be as it is."

"Whose side are you on, anyway?" demanded Wood.

Carla looked first at Trent, then at Wood. "Why... I'm not on anyone's side."

"Well, you'd damn well better get on the side that's paying your salary," growled Wood. "I consider it your duty to convince those people that their fears are groundless, that Baker Labs won't be dirtying their precious community."

"I've told everyone I've talked to that there's no danger of pollution. I think most of them believe me." She'd repeated Trent's assurances several times. It was the other issues that bothered and confused Carla.

"Good," Thorton grumbled, picking up his fork and starting in on his salad. "Let's eat."

The dinner conversation veered away from Roseville and Baker Labs, and Carla was relieved. Thorton Wood was too intense about the subject, and his comments about the residents of Roseville had disturbed her. In fact, the entire evening was becoming a very disturbing experience.

Dan was constantly watching her, to the point of embarrassing her. If she hadn't known better, Carla would have sworn there was a sexual message behind his sidelong glances.

Strange to think she'd once loved him—or thought she loved him. She saw through him now, his always being so careful to agree with Wood, never expressing a controversial opinion of his own. He was even fawning over Trent, laughing at his jokes, feigning close attention to every word he spoke. It was nauseating.

"How about a game of golf tomorrow morning?" Dan suggested to Trent, as they finished their desserts. "I have an eight o'clock tee-off time."

"But you promised to take me!" exclaimed Mary Anne, forcing Dan to finally take notice of her.

It was her father who answered—laughing. "That was a mistake." When Thorton Wood looked at Trent, he was shaking his head. "My experience is that women only hold up play. Sometimes I wonder if they should even be allowed on the course."

Dan nodded in agreement.

"I wouldn't say that around my family," chuckled Trent. "My sister has a lower handicap than most men I know and several years ago my mother was state amateur champion." Then he looked at Dan. "I'm afraid I'll be busy tomorrow."

Mary Anne stared pensively at her coffee, while Carla studied Trent.

He had the advantage tonight. He and the money his company had to invest were being courted. Trent knew why he'd been asked to dinner and why golfing dates were being offered. His attitude was friendly but reserved. Carla liked the easy way he handled himself, not backing down from any position he wished to defend, yet presenting it in a tactful and diplomatic manner.

"Would you like to see the rest of the house?" Thorton asked Trent, as everyone stood to leave the table.

"I'd be delighted."

Trent paused for Carla, but Thorton's next statement stopped her from joining them. "Dan, Carla saw the house last fall. Show her the new advertising layout that's in my study."

It was clear Thorton Wood wanted to be alone with Trent. At Trent's lifted eyebrows, Carla shrugged her shoulders, then followed Dan into Wood's study. Mary Anne started after them, but Dan stopped her with a syrupy sweet order. "Honey, you know how boring you find the banking business. You go on into the living room and I'll be with you just as soon as I can. Oh, and close the door as you leave."

Mary Anne studied the two of them for a moment, sighed, began to close the door, then changed her mind leaving it half open. Dan didn't notice and Carla didn't care.

"It's over here, on his desk," Dan said, strolling across the somber, darkly furnished room to a large oak desk.

Carla glanced through the folder, with its copies of the upcoming advertising layouts. There was September's back-to-school savings promotion, October's fall harvest theme and November's usual Christmas Club reminder. Nothing she had any say about, although the posters would be placed in the Roseville branch in the months to come.

"You look so different tonight," Dan said softly, his warm breath blowing against her cheek, his hand lightly touching her arm.

Carla hadn't realized he was so near and shifted her weight, hoping to put some distance between them. "Same as usual," she mumbled and lifted the arm he'd touched to brush her hair back behind her ear.

"No, you're different. Before you always seemed so reserved, so stand-offish. Tonight you're... you're sexy."

He reached up to stroke her hair, but she turned away from him and moved across the room.

Dan's behavior was confusing her. Surely he wasn't making a pass. Not here in Thorton Wood's study, with Mary Anne in the living room. That would be ridiculous.

Trying to appear at ease, she casually picked up and pretended to be interested in one of Wood's golfing trophies as she said, "Mary Anne's a very nice person. I can see why you like her."

But Dan made no comment, his blue eyes stripping her naked. It was not an experience Carla appreciated or enjoyed.

"You know, there's really nothing I need to know about that advertising campaign. Why don't we join Mary Anne and her mother in the living room." She put down the trophy and started for the door, but before she could make a graceful exit, Dan had crossed the room and stopped her. "Carla, we need to talk."

"Let me go." Her voice was icy as she glared down at the hand on her arm.

"You're still upset with me, aren't you? Just because of that little incident last fall."

"Wouldn't you be upset if you'd been double-crossed by your own fiancé?" She tried to pull her wrist free of his grip but quickly discovered her efforts were only hurting and bruising her arm.

"I did it for you," he said, ignoring her struggle.

Carla stopped fighting and angrily faced him. "Come off it, Dan. You did it for yourself, no one else. You couldn't stand the idea of me being chosen over you, so you lied to Wood."

"I was concerned about your health." Reaching up, he combed his fingers through her hair. "You look lovely tonight, Carla. Radiant. I was a fool to break our engagement. Together we would have made a great team."

"Team?" Carla tried to remember what it was that had made Dan so damned irresistible to her just a year before. No longer did his touch excite her. Even his dashing good looks didn't impress her. Time and experience had cleared her vision. She could see beyond the handsome face to the man—and what she saw, she didn't like. "For just once, Dan, let's be honest. *I* broke the engagement, not you. *You're* the one who lied to Wood. I don't like liars on my team."

"You should have been concerned with my career, should have wanted me to have the job."

He really didn't understand. Carla stared at him for a moment, then sighed. "You should have been supporting my goals, giving me a helping hand—not stabbing me in the back."

"Oh, Carla, I need you," he groaned, suddenly pulling her closer. "I was such a fool."

She was stunned. As Dan's mouth captured hers, one arm tightening around her waist, the other roaming her side to caress a breast, she didn't know what to do. If she made a fuss in her boss's house it would be embarrassing for everyone. Yet she couldn't allow Dan to continue his assault on her.

Before she could come up with a way out of the situation a deep, constrained voice asked from the doorway, "Am I interrupting something?"

Immediately Dan let her go, his eyes darting to

where Trent stood. Carla felt her stomach twist and knew all of the color had drained from her face. Nevertheless, she turned toward Trent. "No, nothing at all."

"I believe the others are waiting for us in the living room. Thorton is serving after-dinner drinks." There was no sign of emotion in Trent's voice.

Carla stepped to his side, her knees quaking but her back straight. One last glance over her shoulder showed Dan had retreated behind the desk and was staring at Trent with an expression of fear.

A slight pressure at the small of her back guided her from the study to the living room. No questions were asked, no accusing comments made, but Carla could feel the tension. Like a time bomb Trent was ready to explode. Meekly Dan followed, keeping a safe distance behind.

Carla sat next to Trent on the couch. His leg touched hers once and she looked at him, needing to know if it had been an intentional caress or an accident. But his expression was guarded, his eyes telling her nothing.

Thorton and Velma described their trip to China, totally unaware of the tension in the room. Carla's right arm ached where Dan had grabbed her. Absently she rubbed the spot only to glance over and catch Trent watching her. Immediately she looked away.

There was no reason to feel guilty. She'd done nothing to be ashamed of. But how would Trent know that? She knew he believed she still had feelings for Dan. What he'd observed in the library was as damaging a bit of evidence as anyone could have planted.

Dan stood behind Mary Anne's chair, his hand touching her shoulder, his fingertips caressing her skin. But Mary Anne wasn't responding. The few comments she directed toward him were distinctly cool, and Carla wondered how much the younger woman knew about what had transpired in the library and how much longer Dan's presence would be welcomed in this household.

They left at ten, Trent promising to keep in touch with Thorton, Carla thanking Velma for a delicious dinner and a lovely evening. In the car she waited for the explosion, but Trent made no mention of the incident. Mile after mile passed, with their conversation touching on every subject but the one that needed to be discussed. Finally she could stand it no longer. "Don't you want to know what was going on in Wood's study?"

"I could see what was going on." His fingers were tightly clenched around the steering wheel, his knuckles nearly white in the moonlight.

"You saw Dan kissing me. Not the other way around."

"It takes two."

"I couldn't get away. He caught me by surprise."

"Do you still love him?" The words were carefully enunciated, and he slowed the car as he waited for her answer.

Reaching over, Carla touched his arm. He had to believe her. "No, I don't love him. Tonight I realized that more than ever. Once I thought Dan was a prince, now I know he's a toad."

"You were upset when you first saw him."

"Because he's always there, trying to worm his way into Wood's good graces. I don't trust him."

Trent glanced her way and she saw his facial muscles relax. "You're sure you're not in love with him?"

"I'm sure."

For a way they traveled in silence, then Trent chuckled, and catching her hand with his, he lifted her fingers to his lips. "A toad, eh?"

"Yes, Thorton. Whatever you say, Thorton," she mimicked.

They both laughed.

The fireflies that flitted along the edge of the road, blinking on and off, were like little gems lighting their way. Carla couldn't remember when she'd felt so relieved or happy. That was, until she recalled how Dan and she had happened to be in the study in the first place. "What went on during your tour of the house?"

"Ah, Thorton and I had a man-to-man talk. He assured me that the Baker Labs accounts would receive special attention if I banked with Indy. That I had only to call, if ever I had any problems."

"What kind of problems does he expect?" Carla bristled. "Doesn't he think I can handle a large investor?"

Trent squeezed her hand. "Don't let it upset you, honey. I'm sure he was simply giving me added assurance. After all, he doesn't know how much confidence I have in you."

"You didn't have much confidence in me a little while ago," Carla reminded him.

"You've got to admit, I did catch you and Dan in a rather awkward situation."

She laughed. "Did you see Dan's face, after he went scurrying behind that desk? I think if you'd taken one step toward him, he would have died right then and there."

"Did you like it?"

"What?" She was still laughing.

"His kiss." Trent had pulled up in front of her house and slammed on the brakes.

Carla braced herself, stopping her forward lunge with a hand on the dash. "Trent Campbell, I might think you were jealous if I didn't know better."

"I'm a very possessive man, Carla. I'll share you with your work, but not with another man."

"I won't be owned."

"I don't want to own you. I want to be your partner."

"But for how long?" she asked, turning in his direction.

"That, my dear, is up to you." He was very serious as he looked at her. "You're going to have a choice to make... one day very soon."

"What choice?" she asked, as he left the car to come around to her side.

"Where your priorities lie. May I come in?"

Before Carla could answer, a high-pitched voice greeted them from across the street. "Lovely night, isn't it? Carla—Mr. Campbell. You two been to Fort Wayne?"

"Business meeting," Carla called back. It was at least a half-truth. "You're up late."

"Couldn't sleep," Miss Atherby called back. "Thought I'd just sit out here and enjoy the evening air for a while."

"She'll be waiting for you to leave," Carla told Trent, as soon as he stepped into her house.

"This is worse than being chaperoned," he groaned.

Catching her face between his hands, he firmly kissed her lips.

"I'm sorry. I know it seems silly, but in a few weeks you'll be gone and I'll still be here."

"That remains to be seen." Lovingly he kissed her entire face not missing a spot. Then he sighed. "All right, tonight's out. Probably just as well. We both need a good night's sleep. But tomorrow, just as soon as you're through work, I get you all to myself."

"I can't," she said, biting her lower lip and leaning her head on his shoulder. "I have to go to Indianapolis. It's my father's birthday. Sort of a family reunion. My sister, her husband, the baby...they'll all be there. I have to go."

"I understand," he murmured, blowing into her hair and gently rubbing her back. "I don't like it, but I understand. What about Sunday?"

"I won't be back until late." She sighed, then looked up at his face. It was crazy, but oh, how she wanted to be with him. "I'm sure this sounds ridiculous, but would you like to come with me?"

The frown that had darkened his features melted away. His lips were warm on hers, his arms strong as they held her close. And when he lifted his head, letting her catch her breath, he was almost laughing. "Yes, I would love to come. What time?"

8

"MOM...DAD...I'D LIKE YOU to meet Trent Campbell."

On the steps of their two-story brick house, Carla's parents stood together—Helen Parker, short and plump, her brown hair streaked with gray; Jay Parker, tall and lean, his hair the same rich chestnut color as Carla's but with a sprinkling of white. While still at the bank, Carla had called her mother and told her Trent would be coming. Now both of her parents studied him curiously. It had been years since she'd brought anyone home for them to meet.

Although Carla's mother said nothing, her brown eyes sparkled. Her father's approval of Trent was more vocal. "Glad to have another man around," he said, shaking Trent's hand.

"That's not fair, dad," a female voice objected from inside the house. "Joe's here."

"Joe's buried in those law books of his and when he isn't he's too tired to talk."

An attractive, medium height, brown-haired, brown-eyed woman stepped out from behind Carla's parents and extended her right hand to Trent. "Hi, I'm Diane, Carla's little sister. And this is J.J.—Joseph Jay Evans." On her left hip Diane balanced a five-month-old baby boy. "As you've gathered, my husband isn't much of a socializer. He's upstairs, studying for his bar exams. But he'll be down for dinner."

"I certainly hope so," her father grunted, stepping back from the door. "Come on in, you two."

When her parents first bought the house in Indianapolis, Carla had thought it too large, but her mother had claimed she'd be cramped in anything smaller. Now, with five adults and a baby in the hallway, the house did seem crowded. Carla's father had no patience for sentimental greetings and, before Carla could even wish him a happy birthday, he escaped to his favorite chair in the living room.

"You're not going to watch baseball all afternoon, are you?" asked his wife, looking first at the back of her husband's head, then at Trent.

"Of course I'm going to watch baseball." Carla's father turned in his chair so he faced them. "I always watch baseball on Saturday afternoons and I'm certainly not going to make an exception on my birthday. I'm sure Carla's friend wants to see this game, too."

Trent looked at Carla, his eyebrow arching slightly.

Her father was an armchair sports fan: spring and summer meant baseball, fall was football and winter was divided between basketball and hockey. For the next few hours her father's attention would be riveted to a twenty-one inch screen, and it sounded as though he expected Trent to share that time with him. "Dad, I think Trent might like to unpack first," Carla suggested, hoping to give Trent an out, if he wanted one.

"Nonsense, he can do that later. You for the Cubs?" he asked Trent.

"I'm a Phillies man, myself," Trent responded, putting the two suitcases he was carrying down by the telephone stand.

"They're not doing badly."

"At least let me show Trent where he's sleeping," tried Carla, sensing her father wasn't about to give up the pleasure of having another man around to watch a game.

"Women," sighed her father, looking at Trent. "Always fussing." A commercial came on and he motioned Carla to his side. "How's my favorite financial expert?" he asked, taking her hand.

"Certainly no expert." Carla leaned down and kissed her dad. "Happy birthday. Feel any older?"

"Eons. But now that you're here, I feel better." He hugged her affectionately.

A little embarrassed, Carla pushed her hair back behind her ear as she stood up, then glanced at Trent, wondering what his reaction might be to the show of affection between father and daughter. Trent winked, and Carla relaxed.

"Your mother fixed up the downstairs for your friend," her father told her, then his attention returned to the television as the game came back on.

"And I'm?"

"Upstairs, across from your sister, Joe and the baby." He groaned as a pop-up fly was caught easily, then looked back at Carla. "At least you're on the same level. Your mother and I are right under them. I swear, your sister walks like an elephant."

"Diane doesn't walk like an elephant, it's the—" Carla started, then shook her head as she realized her father was again absorbed in the game and not listening to her. She motioned to Trent to follow her down the narrow flight of stairs. "Come on, I'll show you where you'll sleep before I lose you to that ball game."

"You won't get rid of me that easily," Trent told her, coming to her side at the bottom of the steps.

The laundry room, water heater and furnace were at the far end of the basement, but to their left was a door that led to a small bedroom. A double bed was flanked by two night stands, an old oak dresser leaned against one wall and a large, oval, braided rug covered the cement floor. The walls were painted a creamy white, while the spread, rug and curtains were in shades of blue. Even the small bathroom, off to the right, had been tiled in blues and white.

"As you can tell, blue is my mother's favorite color," Carla commented as Trent put his suitcase down and closed the door. "Mom and dad moved here five years ago when dad was promoted. They only use this room when they have a house full of guests, so I don't know how comfortable the bed will be."

"Want to give it a test run?" Trent's eyebrows lifted and before Carla could answer, he had her in his arms and they both fell across the bed.

"Trent Campbell!" she gasped, in a voice just barely above a whisper. "What are you...?"

His mouth silenced the rest as he rolled on top of her. For a moment she struggled, laughing and pushing with her hands, then she stopped, her lips moving with his, her arms wrapping around his back. Only when she was totally responsive did Trent lift his head. "I've been wanting to do that ever since I picked you up at your house."

"And I've been wanting you to do it." She sighed,

running her fingers through his golden brown hair.

"You know, you look a lot like your father." Slowly Trent's fingertips traced the curve of her jaw, followed the graceful line of her neck down to her shoulders, then moved over the front of her white cotton blouse. "However, you do have a few more curves than your father."

"I certainly hope so." She could feel her nipple harden as he cupped the palm of his hand over her breast. "Also dad's eyes are blue."

Leaning forward, Trent kissed each of her eyelids, then murmured near her ear, "Personally, I like the way yours change color."

"That's the woman in me, dad always says. Can't make up my mind whether to have green eyes or brown."

"Hmm, I think the woman in you is a little lower." Suggestively Trent rubbed his hips against hers, his arousal evident, and Carla felt a tingling start between her legs.

"Dad expects you to watch the game with him," she whispered, as much to remind herself as Trent.

"I can think of something I'd rather do than watch baseball."

"Oh, Trent, I hope you're not bored today. My father's a real sports nut and thinks everyone else should be, too."

"I like sports," he said, unbuttoning the top button of her blouse. "How about a team effort?"

"Trent, stop!" Carla cried, as he released two more buttons. "I'm not kidding. Dad will be down here any minute, wondering why you're not dying to see how the Cubs are doing."

"I swear, where you're concerned, I'm doomed to

a life of frustration.'' Trent groaned, then reluctantly levered himself off the bed and gave her a hand up. ''I don't suppose I'll get any time with you tonight?''

''I don't know.'' Carla quickly rebuttoned her blouse, then checked her hair in the mirror. Her long tresses were tangled, and she ran her fingers through them. But there was little she could do about the well-kissed look of her lips.

Turning to face him, Carla watched Trent tuck his blue-and-gold striped polo shirt back into his gray slacks. She did want to be with him. ''My parents usually go to bed early. Maybe after everyone's asleep....'' She wondered if she'd have the nerve to slip downstairs past her parents' bedroom. Strange how childhood inhibitions remained.

''At least there's hope.'' Trent smiled and took her hand. Together they went back up the stairs.

''Wondered when you two were coming back,'' her father commented, briefly looking up when they entered the living room. ''Thought I was going to have to come get you. Helen brought you a beer,'' he told Trent. ''You going to watch the game?'' he asked Carla.

''Maybe later, I should go in and visit with mom and Diane for a while.'' With a smile of regret Carla left Trent with her father and went into the kitchen.

For over two hours Carla chatted with her mother and sister. That was, when Helen Parker wasn't jumping up, waiting on her father and Trent, bringing them fresh beers, crackers and cheese.

Nothing had changed. Her mother subjugated her will to that of her husband's. It irritated Carla, but she'd learned long ago nothing she said made any difference. The woman seemed to enjoy her role.

Bouncing J.J. on her knee, Carla entertained her little nephew, making faces and playing games of peek-a-boo. She winced, then laughed as the baby caught a hank of her hair and gave it a jerk. "J.J., you're a brute, but a lovable one. If your mama's not careful, I may just take you home with me."

"Now that would set the tongues wagging in Roseville," Trent commented from the kitchen doorway.

Carla looked up to find him watching her. How long he'd been there she didn't know, but her heart skipped a beat when their eyes met. Frustration etched its way through her body, a fine line of tension that put her on edge. She wanted to be with him, all alone, just the two of them—but, at the moment, that was impossible.

"Tying run's on third base," her father yelled from the living room. "Better get back in here, Trent."

Trent smiled before he returned to the living room, and Carla knew he shared her feelings. Thursday night now seemed like a dream. She would find a way to his room tonight, no matter what.

"DELICIOUS DINNER." Trent complimented Carla's mother as he finished the last bite of his steak and reached for his coffee.

"As usual, Mother Parker," Joe seconded.

Trent and Joe had gotten along well, especially after Trent mentioned some legal battles Campbell Industries had been involved in. "Corporate law is my specialty," Joe told Trent, and for a long while the topic of law monopolized the conversation, until Carla's father broke in.

"You missed a good game this afternoon, Joe, even though the Cubs did lose."

J.J. banged on the highchair and squealed in delight when Carla's mother brought out a two-layer chocolate cake with candles. Happy birthday was sung, Trent's deep voice blending in with the others. Her father made a show of indifference but he enjoyed every minute of being in the limelight. There were several gifts for him to open. Even Trent had a present for her father, and Carla knew her dad was impressed by the gold-plated pen and pencil set. "Thank you, son," he said, shaking Trent's hand.

Rising to his feet after the cake and ice cream were finished, her father looked around the table and for an instant Carla thought of a patriarch presiding over his clan. The similarity seemed especially fitting when he began giving orders. "Helen and Diane can clear the table. Carla...Trent, you come with me. Joe, I presume you'll be studying."

"Have to, dad."

Everyone went in their assigned directions. Joe returned upstairs taking the baby with him. Carla's mother and Diane began to clear the table, and Trent and Carla followed her father outside.

"I'm worried about your mother," her father began, as soon as the three of them were seated on the wicker chairs on the porch. "If I should die tomorrow, she wouldn't know what to do."

"Dad, you're only fifty-eight," Carla laughed. "You're hardly going to keel over tomorrow."

"Don't laugh," her father admonished. "It happens all the time, especially to men my age. Don't forget, dear, I'm in the insurance business. I see the statistics."

"And you also know heredity plays an important part in those statistics. You come from a line of longevity. Grandpa's still going strong, and he's eighty-three."

"I could be hit by a car tomorrow." He glared at his daughter.

"All right, you could die tomorrow," she admitted, seeing he was serious about the matter. "What's the problem, dad? You've got insurance, haven't you?"

"Of course I have insurance. More than enough to see your mother comfortably through the rest of her life. But that's what worries me. Your mother has no head for money. She might squander it on clothes... invest in some get-rich scheme... marry the first man who comes along. Who knows!" He shook his head.

"Mom has more sense than you're giving her credit for. She isn't going to run off with the first man who comes along or throw away money she knows she needs. Besides, if anything did happen to you, Diane and I would keep an eye on mom."

"I know that, but you're the levelheaded one, Carla. You always have been. You don't let yourself get carried away by your emotions, like your sister does. If something happens to me, I want you to take care of your mother."

"Dad, stop talking like something is going to happen."

"Carla." He spoke her name sharply.

"All right, I will, dad," she sighed. It was something she might have to face one day, but unless her father did have an accident, he would probably live for a long, long time.

"I knew   could depend on you.' He patted ner hand, then stood and stretched. "There's an old war movie on tonight, Trent. John Wayne. They don't make men like him anymore. Want to come in and watch it with me?"

"I think Carla and I might take a walk," Trent said, also standing.

Her father looked at her, then Trent. With a knowing grin he went into the house.

"You've certainly met with his approval," Carla told Trent, as they strolled along the sidewalk.

"I'm glad. Your father seems very concerned about dying. Has he been ill?"

"No." Carla halfsmiled. "For the past few years I've gone through this in some form or another every birthday. Adding another year makes Dad despondent, but it seems to pass as soon as the day ends. It just always irritates me that he doesn't have more faith in mom—or Diane. Not that I wouldn't watch over mom. That goes without saying."

"I've noticed your mother caters to your father. Has she always?"

"Caters! She waits on him hand and foot." Carla snorted in an unladylike manner.

"And you don't like that?"

"No, I don't."

They walked in silence for a few minutes. Then Trent said, "Having met your parents, a lot of little things you've said and done make sense now."

"Such as?"

"Such as your statement against hiring a maid. You said it was demeaning. But it was your mother you were talking about, wasn't it?"

"Nonsense." She turned her back to him and stared at the house across the street.

"And your father. You said he'd wanted a son. You became that son, didn't you? You became logical, prudent, career-minded Carla."

"That's ridiculous," she snapped, spinning back to face him. "Do I look like a man?"

Trent smiled. "Not today, but the woman I met last week wasn't far from that image—tailored clothes, severe hairdo, initials on the door. And it's interesting that you hate cooking, sewing and housework. All the things that are typically feminine."

"You like to cook and sew. Does that make you a woman?"

"Not at all . . . and what you do doesn't make you a man. . . . But I'm not afraid of the masculine side of my personality."

"You're jumping to conclusions."

"Am I?"

"Yes."

"I think not. I think you saw your mother catering to your father and decided, as a child, that to be feminine was to be weak. You're afraid of being dominated by a man. That's probably why you've never married."

"I was engaged, if you'll recall. Dan and I planned on being married."

"Makes sense. He would have been no threat to you. He wouldn't have dominated you. Toads don't give orders."

"Who do you think you are, anyway? I invite you here to help celebrate my father's birthday and you insult my parents—and me. You think you know me. Well, you don't! And I don't have to stand here and listen to your two-bit psychoanalysis." Fuming, she turned on her heel and stormed back to her parents' house.

Trent followed, but didn't attempt to catch or stop her. The screen door slammed behind her when she entered the house and Carla ran up the stairs without a word to anyone. In her room she cried out her anger.

If this was love, it hurt too much. Trent was stripping away all of her defenses, forcing her to look at herself with a critical eye. And she didn't like at all what she saw.

It wasn't until much later that she came back downstairs. No one noticed when she stopped in the hallway and looked into the living room. Her father was in his usual chair, watching John Wayne lead his troops into victory. Trent was seated on the couch beside Diane. Her mother was rocking slowly in the old rocking chair, sewing a button on one of her father's shirts. Carla didn't join them. Instead she studied her father's profile.

She loved her father—there was no denying that—but she wondered if things would have been different—if *she* might have been different—if Jay Parker hadn't so desperately wanted to have a son.

Even as a young child she'd read the subtle messages, the comments he made to other men, the envy he had of those with sons, and the pleasure he showed when she was aggressive and competitive, especially if she won. She was intelligent and had learned quickly how to gain his favor. She had felt that even though she couldn't be a boy she could try to be as good as one.

Her sister had never wanted her father's approval as badly as she had, had never been as competitive; it simply wasn't Diane's nature. Carla sighed as she watched her sister pass a bowl of popcorn to Trent. Diane had always been content to be just exactly who she was—a bright, thoughtful girl—and now her sister was happy in her role as wife and mother.

Wife and mother. Strange, those words had always sounded demeaning before, but since meeting Trent....

A warm glow surged through her as she let her eyes linger on the back of his head. Perhaps she would like to be a wife, have children and keep house. Perhaps, with the right man, being a housewife could be a pleasure.

Her gaze moved to her mother.

Carla watched Helen Parker tie off a thread and carefully snip it close to the button she was working on. Then her mother held up her father's shirt and gave it one final check before setting it aside.

For the first time in her life Carla could understand why her mother did so much for her father. He never demanded her servitude; she simply gave and he accepted. Love was the motivation; love was the result. Maybe her mother was not a "liberated" woman, but in her own way she was stronger than any of them.

A tear slipped down Carla's cheek. All of those years she'd judged her mother so harshly, condemned her and vowed never to be like her. It seemed she had a lot to learn.

When the movie ended, Trent rose from the couch and faced her. But Carla lowered her eyes. She wasn't ready to talk to him. Not yet. "I'll see you in the morning," he muttered as he passed and she nodded.

"'Night dad, mom," she said, giving her mother a hug before going up the stairs with her sister. "'Night Diane," she whispered, as they parted in the hallway.

Diane quietly opened the door to her room, showing Joe asleep on the bed, an open book on his lap, the baby curled up beside him. "So much for studying," her sister whispered back. "See you in the morning."

In bed Carla couldn't sleep. Tossing and turning, she rehashed her argument with Trent and tried to honestly evaluate her childhood. What had once been clearly black and white, now appeared gray. For so many years she'd misconstrued her mother's behavior and idolized her father. Now, as an adult, she realized her error.

Again she cried, and when there were no more tears, she felt drained. Her head was throbbing and she finally got up.

Slipping on her robe, Carla opened her bedroom door and tiptoed past her sister's room. The house was dark and quiet, only an occasional snore disturbing the silence. A stair creaked when Carla stepped on it and she paused for a moment, not wanting to waken anyone and have them see her puffy, red-rimmed eyes.

Her parents' door was closed, as usual. In the kitchen the glare of the light made her head ache even more. Quickly she headed for the sink.

Two aspirins with a glass of water were her first priority. Then she splashed cold water over her face, washing away the tear stains and calming her irritated eyes. She was wiping her face with a towel when a deep voice asked, "Can't sleep?"

Carla gasped, her hand going to her mouth, then she let out her breath. "You scared me, Trent. What are you doing up?"

He stood in the doorway, his hair rumpled, his chest and feet bare, only his gray slacks covering his lower half. "I was still awake. When I heard footsteps, I thought I'd come up and see if it was you." His eyes held hers. "I'm sorry."

"I'm sorry, too," she murmured.

His long strides took him quickly across the room and she willingly went into his arms, finding comfort in the warmth of his embrace. "I don't want to fight with you," he said.

"It...it was all so silly." Tears began to form again and Carla blinked her eyes, her long lashes glistening. "I shouldn't have gotten as upset as I did."

"Let's go downstairs, where we can talk without disturbing anyone." Taking her hand, he led the way.

Trent closed the bedroom door behind them, then walked over to his rumpled bed and sat down. Fluffing the pillow behind his back, he stretched his legs out over the sheet, then patted the spot beside him. Carla joined him, sitting shoulder to shoulder, her nightgown hiked up to her knees.

He reached over and turned off the bed lamp. Carla closed her eyes and leaned back against the headboard. Her head still ached, but the pain was less intense.

"I never should have criticized you—or your parents," Trent began, taking her hand in his. "I had no right."

"You were too close to the truth, that was the problem," she confessed. "I guess I'm a classic example of a father-daughter complex. You were right. I tried to be that son he always said he wanted.

"When I was younger, I was a regular tomboy. In high school I even took to wearing my hair short and dressed in jeans and plain colored tops. Then one day I heard a group of boys talking about me. They didn't know I was there and what they said was terrible. After that, I let my hair grow long and started wearing dresses. But I just didn't want to be like my mother." Carla took a deep cleansing breath before continuing. "Now I realize that wouldn't be all bad. I envy my sister. She has a beautiful relationship with Joe."

"There's no reason why you can't have that, too," Trent reassured her. His arm went around her shoulders and he pulled her closer, his mouth finding hers.

He kissed her face and neck in a dozen little places, each more stimulating than the last. His hand slid over the nylon of her robe and nightgown, pressing the lilac-colored material against her breasts until the darker hue of her aureoles showed through the two filmy layers.

Before Carla knew it, Trent had removed her robe and gown and cast them aside, along with his slacks. "I don't want to dominate you," he breathed near her ear. "I want to be a part of your life."

"But for how long?" she groaned.

"That I can't answer, honey. Only time will tell."

Again he kissed her and Carla put aside all thoughts of the future. He was with her, here and now, taking her on an erotic journey, and she was eager to follow.

Expertly Trent guided her along the way, using words to excite her, his hands to direct her. They explored every avenue of pleasure, the tip of his tongue skimming like fire across her skin, his fingers awakening new worlds of sensation. She'd thought it had been wonderful before—when they'd made love for the first time—but now he knew her, knew how to take her to the edge, then bring her back, extending their pilgrimage.

His roving hands found their quest and the route became one traveled since the beginnings of mankind. Together they progressed as one, their limbs entwined. "Yes, oh, yes," Carla cried out, mindless of anything she was saying, knowing only that Trent had found that perfect spot. His own convulsions extended her pleasure and gave her the assurance of knowing she'd also satisfied him.

And when it was over, they lay exhausted in each other's arms. Too dazed to talk, Carla merely stroked his damp body, marveling at his supple muscles. For one so strong, he was a gentle, giving man. And she loved him. Oh, how she loved him.

"They're right. Making up is worth the battle," he murmured, brushing a lock of damp hair out of her eyes. "I feel like John Wayne. I could take on the world, save the universe for mankind ... or womankind."

Carla laughed. "My father would approve."

Trent sobered, stroking her hair, leaning on one elbow to gaze at her. "I hope you know how much you mean to me."

Burying her face against his chest, she breathed in

the scent of him. She didn't know, she could only hope. With him she had discovered how wonderful it felt to be a woman in love with a man who gave as much as he took. "Could I interest you in a repeat performance?" she asked innocently, her fingers moving down between his legs.

"Whoa, honey," he gasped, catching her hand. "Even John Wayne needs a few minutes."

But he kissed her and stroked her body. And when he was ready, he made love to her with a tender passion that carried her beyond anything she'd ever experienced. It was early in the morning before she tiptoed back up to her bedroom.

9

OVER THE NEXT TWO WEEKS Carla was with Trent as much as propriety and their work schedules would allow. Twice he flew to Philadelphia to confer with his father and the corporation's board of directors, but if he was in or around Roseville at noon he took her out to lunch. In the evenings they would either go out to dinner or Trent would cook, Carla fixing the salad or helping him prepare the main course.

Saturday night they went to a concert at the Foellinger Theater in Fort Wayne, Sunday to church, then a visit to the Old Fort Wayne fort, going back in time to the early nineteenth century. During the week the evening hours were spent in talk, playing checkers or reading. Trent always left her house by eleven, and Miss Atherby herself commented that he was certainly a proper gentleman.

"Little does she know what goes on in my bedroom between nine and eleven," laughed Carla. It was Thursday night and Trent had decided to prepare fettuccine.

"Now, be fair. There were a couple of nights when all you received was a chaste kiss," he reminded her.

"Because you preferred reading those boring drainage reports all evening."

"I had no choice. Could you hand me the Parmesan, please?"

"Yes, dear. Right away, dear." She imitated a servile attitude and Trent frowned, catching her hand as she handed him the cheese.

"Never, Miss Parker. You and I are equals. Understood?"

With a teasing grin Carla twisted away from his grasp. "If we're so equal, why do I have to listen to all of the people complaining about your chemical plant, while you run around the countryside or fly off to Philadelphia?"

"What I've been doing since I came to Roseville hasn't been all fun and games. And I've heard some of the arguments. It's just that the people around here feel freer talking to you. They know you. They trust you. To them, I'm still a stranger."

"*Some* trust me," she corrected, slicing fresh zucchini and summer squash. "Others view bankers almost as suspiciously as they do owners of chemical plants. You're going to have a lot of opposition at that zoning meeting Tuesday."

"I know, but your support will help. That salad ready?"

During dinner she reiterated all of the complaints she'd heard against the idea of a chemical plant coming to Roseville. It was better to prepare him for the worst, Carla reasoned. And the more debate she listened to, the less convinced she was that Baker Labs would be good for Roseville. It was an opinion she hadn't yet voiced to Trent. The ramifications of that decision were more than she was presently ready to face.

"I'M GOING TO BE GONE for a few days," Trent told her later that night, as they lay on her bed pleasantly exhausted from their lovemaking.

"Why didn't you tell me before?" Carla sat up, already sensing a loss.

"I didn't want to spoil tonight. I'm driving to Chicago in the morning. I need to talk to the managers of the plant, let our engineers look over the reports I have and get some statistics from our PR men. From what you've told me, I'm going to need all the help I can get at that zoning meeting."

"When will you be back?" She'd been looking forward to spending the weekend with Trent. It seemed the time they had together always went too quickly.

"Sometime Monday." Lightly his fingertips moved over her back. "Will you miss me?"

"Of course I'll miss you," she confessed, turning and fitting herself into the circle of his arms.

They made love again—desperately, passionately—not wanting to part. His leaving reminded her of the one thing she wanted to ignore. Soon Trent's work would be finished in Roseville. No matter which way the vote went Tuesday night, Trent wouldn't be staying. He had other companies to tend to, other problems to tackle. If Baker Labs did come to Roseville she would see him occasionally. But would that be enough?

Trent called twice that weekend and the sound of his voice made the separation tolerable. "Carla," he said Sunday evening, "I'll be back in Roseville tomorrow, and I've decided I'm ready to brave your steaks. They can't be all that bad."

"You must be sick if you're willing to try my cooking," she laughed.

"I'll bring the wine and the antacids."

"Darn it, Trent, I can't. It's the first Monday of the

month. Wood always holds his staff meetings the first Monday night of each month."

"How late will you be?" Trent sounded tired and disappointed.

"It depends on Wood and how much material he decides to go over. Maybe ten . . . maybe eleven."

"Come by my place when you're through. I'll fix you a drink and we can discuss your assets."

Liabilities would be more accurate, Carla thought. She was beginning to wonder if she would be a help or a hindrance to Trent at the zoning meeting. The arguments she'd been hearing against Baker Labs were beginning to make sense.

Oh, not all of them. Some were emotional, frightened responses to something new and unknown. But much of the reasoning for keeping the chemical plant out of Roseville was sound and, despite her earlier enthusiasm, Carla agreed—Baker Labs should not come to Roseville.

But how to tell Trent? And how would he react? She knew from experience how irrational Dan had become when she opposed him. Carla wasn't certain if she wanted to risk losing Trent for the sake of a town.

WOOD ASKED HER TO STAY after the meeting and, as soon as the room was empty, began to impress on her how important Baker Labs was for Indy Bank. "I didn't want to say anything in front of Campbell the night the two of you were over," Wood said, lighting a cigar and rising from his chair, "but Dan is right. Roseville is a dying town. If the vote is against Baker Labs tomorrow night I see no alternative but to close the Roseville branch."

"You can't," cried Carla, also rising to her feet. There were so many older people in and around Roseville who depended on the bank's services.

"I not only can, I will." Thorton Wood straightened to his full height, then frowned as he found himself looking directly at Carla's chin. "Banking is a business, not a service organization. The farmers and businessmen around Roseville will simply have to drive a little farther to make their deposits."

"We could cut our hours, release one teller." She was thinking of all the cost cutting moves they could initiate. "Roseville needs a bank. The senior citizens—"

"We cannot afford to keep a bank open for a handful of people." Wood cut her off as he jammed his cigar out in an ashtray on the table.

At a loss for words, Carla turned away and stared out the window. The fifteenth floor conference room offered her a view of Fort Wayne. Streetlights mapped out the city and were reflected in its rivers, while cars moving along one-way streets created flickering patterns of red and white. Blinking yellow lights warned of construction areas. Fort Wayne was busy, growing and constantly changing. That's why it could support six full-service banks and four savings and loan associations.

"And if Baker Labs does come to Roseville?" The idea caused her to sigh inadvertently.

"The bank stays, of course. With two thousand employees, that plant will completely change Roseville."

"I know." She turned back to face him. "If the zoning change isn't approved and you do close the bank, what about my job?"

"At present we don't have any openings for a manager, but you're a good worker, Carla. There'll always be a place for you with Indy."

A place. Probably as an assistant manager. Not exactly the step forward that she'd planned. "I understand," she said. "Is there anything else I should know?"

"No, that's all." But before she left the conference room, he stopped her with one last statement. "I expect you to attend that meeting tomorrow night, Carla. And, if necessary, talk that town into giving Campbell his variance. Anything less won't be enough. Do you understand what I mean?"

She did. Baker Labs was becoming a very personal matter. If she supported the chemical plant, she would see Trent once in a while, the bank would remain open, grow, and her chances of becoming a vice-president would improve. But if she supported those who wanted to keep Roseville as it was—a friendly, cozy, little rural town—Trent, the bank and any chance of a promotion would be lost.

"How's my favorite bank manager?" asked Trent, taking her into his arms and kissing her as soon as she arrived at his door. Then he let her go and studied her closely. "You look tired. Long meeting?"

"Long enough," she sighed, kicking off her heels and walking into his living room. Sinking down on the couch, she leaned her head back and began to rub her temples.

"I'll fix you a drink. A glass of wine all right?" he asked, going into the kitchen.

"Anything," she called, trying to ease the tension building within her.

He returned with two glasses of Pinot Blanc, and Carla took several sips of hers, welcoming its relaxing effect. Sitting beside her, Trent began to massage her neck and back and she leaned forward, grateful for the gentle strengh of his hands.

"What happened?" Trent asked at length.

"I was told, rather bluntly, to vocally support Baker Labs tomorrow night, that if your bid for rezoning failed, Roseville would be without a bank and I would be back in Fort Wayne as an assistant manager."

"You're kidding." Trent paused a minute, then seeing she was serious, rubbed her shoulders even more vigorously. "Why is it so important to Wood that Baker Labs come to Roseville?"

"It's a matter of finance," Carla replied. "I knew our profits were low, but I thought we were operating enough in the black to keep us open. Wood disagrees. He says he can't afford to run a service organization."

She took a deep breath and set down her glass. The time had come to be honest. "Trent, I don't want the bank to close, I don't want to lose my job as manager and I don't want to lose you, but I'm not sure if I can support the rezoning."

Rising to her feet, she left Trent on the couch. Now that she'd mentioned her qualms, she had to tell him her reasons. "Maybe Roseville is just a small town, but it's special. Here people know each other, care about each other. Here people take the time to stop and talk. And I can walk down these streets, day or night, and not worry about being mugged or raped. How many women can say that who live in a city?"

As she paced back and forth her hands moved through the air, emphasizing her statements. "Sure, Roseville's unsophisticated and perhaps a little dull, but the people here are honest and trustworthy." She stopped her pacing and faced Trent, pointing an accusing finger his way. "Do you realize what will happen to this town if your plant comes here?"

Before Trent could answer, Carla began to list the consequences. "There would be new houses, hundreds of them, built on good, productive farmland, and there would be roads, with lots of pavement, over that same rich soil. And new people would move in." She stopped Trent before he could interrupt.

"Oh, I know. Most of them would be highly educated people. But don't you see, that's even worse. They would bring their way of life here. They wouldn't assimilate, they'd dominate. And the Bob Dolmans, and Ken Pierces and Neil Higginses would all be out of business because their cute little country stores and gas stations wouldn't be able to survive."

"Carla, change is inevitable," Trent finally managed to get in.

"Sure, change is, but not this big a change. Not the changes two thousand people would bring. Besides your plant, other businesses would come—shopping malls, factories. And they'd bring even more people and houses. Soon Roseville as we know it would be gone. In its place there would simply be another suburb of Fort Wayne. The farms would be housing tracts, our country roads highways."

"I thought you wanted Roseville to grow?" said Trent.

Carla sighed, drained by her emotional outburst. "I thought I did, too."

"And now you've changed your mind?" Trent downed his wine, still watching her. The tension she was under was evident in her jerky motions.

"I don't know what to think." She shook her head, wondering how she could even consider opposing Trent—the man she loved. "I'm tired and confused. All day long I've listened to objections to your plant. Then tonight, with Wood—"

He rose to his feet and came to her side. "Carla, I hate to see you this upset." His arms went around her and he gathered her close, his lips touching her forehead. "I didn't realize Wood was putting pressure on you."

"It isn't just Wood." Tears were welling in her eyes and it was difficult for her to keep them under control. "Trent, I want to support you, I want to assure everyone that Baker Labs is the best thing that could possibly happen to Roseville. But I don't know if it is." The last came out as a choked sob.

"Hey," he murmured, kissing the salty drops from her cheeks. "Don't cry, honey. I know how important your career is to you and I know what I want, but I'm also sure you'll weigh all sides carefully before you make your decision. I have confidence in you. You'll make the right choice."

"But which one is the right choice?" she moaned.

"That, you'll have to decide," he whispered, holding her tight. He nibbled on her earlobe, his hands beginning to wander over her back and down her sides.

A surging warmth filled her body, but sex was not

the answer. No matter how good Trent made her feel in bed, it wouldn't solve the dilemma she now faced. "Don't," Carla groaned, pulling back.

Trent seemed surprised and she took in a deep breath, trying to calm the quiver in the pit of her stomach. "I'm sorry, but it's late and I'm tired. Suddenly I don't know what I want or how I feel. I think the best thing for me to do is go home and get a good night's sleep."

BUT SLEEP DIDN'T COME that easily. For hours she paced the floor, doing exactly as Trent had said she would. She weighed every factor and looked at all sides, and when she was finished she still didn't know what to do. Emotionally she concurred with the townspeople who opposed the plant. That was the problem. It was an emotional response, not a logical one. Three weeks before she wouldn't have had any problems making up her mind. The old Carla Parker wouldn't have been swayed by emotion. That Carla Parker dealt in facts and figures—dollars and cents. And those figures clearly favored the building of Baker Labs in Roseville.

Back and forth she seesawed, trying to make up her mind. In the end, the best solution seemed to be, to do and say nothing. Despite Wood's orders, she would remain neutral.

In all fairness she wanted to tell Trent that she'd decided not to speak during the meeting, but she didn't get the chance. Trent didn't come to the bank or stop by at lunch or after work, and every time Carla tried calling him, there was no answer. Where he was, she didn't know.

The meeting was being held in the high school

gymnasium. By seven-thirty cars already filled the parking lot and were beginning to line the road. A few people, Carla included, walked to the school, enjoying the balmy evening air.

A van with a Fort Wayne television station's call letters on its side was parked outside the school. The debate over a chemical plant coming to Roseville had become newsworthy. All week the Fort Wayne newspapers had carried articles, while the television stations had interviewed Roseville's residents. Felix Gordon had published another special edition of the *Sun*, printing letters to the editor both for and against the chemical plant. The town was clearly divided. Tonight it would be up to the zoning board to make the decision.

Inside the gym Carla looked for Trent, but he wasn't to be found among those in the room. The size of the crowd surprised her and there were others milling about in the hallway. The importance of the meeting was evident.

"Can you believe it?" asked Bob Dolman, coming up beside her. "I don't think Roseville's seen this many people since Kennedy stopped by here in 1960."

"Have you seen Trent?" asked Carla, beginning to get concerned.

"Oh, he'll be around. Hey, there's Phil Goodman, of the *Gazette*. I want to talk to him." And he was off, weaving his way through the crowd.

It was nearly eight, and time for the meeting. The room was filling quickly, the noise increasing. Carla found a chair midway from the front near the center and sat down as a gavel began to resound, its sharp raps rising above the noise. As all of the men and women in the room took their seats the chatter lessened until at last the chairman of the board could be heard.

"Ladies...gentlemen...please...if you'll all be quiet we can get this meeting under way."

It was then Trent entered the room, along with Felix Gordon, who was carrying a wooden easel. Trent had his arms filled with eighteen- by twenty-four-inch sheets of white poster board. He nodded his thanks when Felix had set up the easel. Then he placed the placards on the easel and sat down.

"If we are ready," the chairman began and read the proposed zoning change.

Immediately there was an uproar and again the sound of the gavel echoed throughout the gym.

Trent glanced around the room during the disturbance, his calm expression giving no indication if he was perturbed by the clamor. He looked distinguished and assured in his brown suit, cotton shirt and striped tie. Even the heat, growing more and more uncomfortable in the crowded room, seemed to be having no effect on him.

Then their eyes met and Carla's pulse quickened, her own smile reflected in his. She gazed at him, trying to hold, at least for a moment longer, the unity they still shared. Then the chairman had order and Trent looked away.

"First we'll hear from Mr. Campbell, then there will be ample opportunity for questions and comments. Mr. Campbell."

Trent stood and smiled as he looked over the mixed group of men and women in front of him. There were old and young, college graduates and high school dropouts, farmers, businessmen, career women and housewives. Some smiled warmly, wanting the prosperity, the jobs and the progress Baker Labs would bring to Roseville. Others eyed Trent cautiously, reserving judgment. One group, however, was openly antagonistic. A woman at the back of the room waved a sign with the words *Don't Forget Love Canal.*

"Some of you I've met, others I haven't," Trent began, standing next to the easel. "I know from talking to you, reading your letters to the editor and listening to those interviewed on television that there is a lot of concern about environmental safety."

"With good reason!" a man shouted, rising to his feet and shaking a fist at Trent. "Look at what...." His words were drowned out by a chorus of voices.

Carla cringed. Would Trent even get a chance to talk?

But the chairman banged his gavel and those sitting near the man pulled him back down into his chair.

"Let me begin by giving you a little background on Baker Labs," Trent continued.

Calmly, systematically, he described the chemical plant, its products and finally its methods of dealing with dangerous chemical waste. "Our past record is excellent, our future positive. New advancements have produced a method of bonding chemical waste in a way to render it harmless. It can be stored on site with no danger of leaking into the soil, getting into the water system or polluting the atmosphere."

He turned to the posters on the easel. Artist-enhanced photographs, graphs and diagrams all visually reinforced Trent's statements. "I think all of you would agree, chemical products are here to stay.

Your fields wouldn't produce half the yield they do now without weed killers, bug sprays and fertilizers. And in your homes chemicals clean your toilets, clear your drains and keep out pests. But there's no reason why a chemical plant has to destroy the environment. Baker Labs has proven that. What Baker Labs is offering Roseville is economic growth, jobs for your unemployed and increased tax money for improved roads and better schools.''

When Trent finished talking there was a general murmur of approval. Carla relaxed in her chair. He was a dynamic speaker with a charisma that drew people to him. Looking around the room, she could tell those who had been undecided were favorably impressed.

The initial questions asked by the audience all dealt with environmental safety and Trent's answers lay each of the concerns to rest. It seemed, at that point, that Trent had the zoning variance won. Even the most stalwart of his opponents had begun to be swayed. Then Alice Higgins stood up.

"I know so far most of the concerns people have been voicing are pollution, Mr. Campbell,'' she began. "What I'd like to know is, is it true that Baker Labs will employ two thousand workers?''

"One day, yes.''

Before Trent could go on, Alice continued. "In that case, Mr. Campbell, have you considered how that is going to affect our community?''

She brought up the points about the loss of farmland to new housing and highways; the fundamental changes a rapid growth in population would create in the community and schools; and, basically, the loss of a way of life.

Trent addressed himself to each point. Carla could tell her emotional speech the night before had prepared him. Others in the room raised questions— some on taxes, some on job opportunities. When there was a lull, Carla wasn't really certain which way the zoning board would vote.

"Anyone else?" asked the chairman, glancing around the gym. "Miss Parker, what about you?" he asked, his eyes stopping at her chair. "What are the views of our banker?"

Carla shifted uneasily in her seat, cleared her throat and looked at Trent. She wished she could have talked to him earlier, told him of her decision. Now it was too late. She was on the spot. She had to say something whether she'd planned it or not; however, she could keep her comments general, not actually state whether she supported the variance or not. Slowly she rose to her feet.

"As many of you know, over the past few weeks I've gotten to know Mr. Campbell quite well."

There was a chuckle from the audience and Carla could feel the color rising to her cheeks, but she went on. "I have learned he is an honest, hardworking man. When he starts a project, he is thorough, efficient and precise. I have also checked up on Baker Labs and what he has told you about their environmental safety record is correct."

Again she cleared her throat. Absently she touched the collar of her blue cotton shirtdress to make certain it was straight. Her hair was purposely pulled up in a knot as a reminder to herself that she was indeed a bank manager and had an obligation to Indy Bank and Trust.

"As your banker, I can assure you that Baker Labs

would be a financial asset to this community. The census reports clearly show that Roseville's population has been declining at a steady rate over the last twenty years. The empty businesses in town indicate the problem that all of our merchants are facing. Roseville is dying and unless new business comes into the area—more people—in another ten years there won't be much of a town left. Baker Labs would solve that problem."

She was going to leave it at that—facts, not emotion, would have been her presentation—but Miss Atherby stood and faced her. "Carla, dear," the older woman began, "I know you know Mr. Campbell well and I'm certain you have a good grasp of the working of his company, but you also know this town. In your opinion, what affect will Baker Labs have on Roseville?"

Carla looked at Trent, her heart caught in her throat. This wasn't the way she wanted it. She'd intended to make her statement, then sit down. Now she was trapped.

Trent's gaze was steady. He knew her ambivalence, yet no warning flashed from his eyes and no scowl darkened his features. Taking hold of the back of the chair in front of her, Carla drew in a deep breath, then slowly exhaled it as she answered Cora Atherby. "I think it would be disastrous."

There was an uproar and immediately the chairman began to bang his gavel. Carla looked at Trent. He was watching her, his arms folded across his chest—not smiling, not frowning—just watching. What he was thinking, she could only guess. Whatever his feelings, he was not about to express them in public.

At last the chairman had order. "Go on, Carla," he said.

"There is nothing wrong with Baker Labs," Carla continued. "It will be an asset to any city. *City*," she repeated, "not farm community. Roseville needs to grow, but slowly, gradually. We need small businesses and factories that employ a few dozen or a couple of hundred workers. That's what you businessmen should be trying to attract to Roseville. That way the community would assimilate the new, and change would be slow and natural."

She went on, and by the time she was finished Carla felt drained. When she sank down in her chair she barely heard the approving comments of those around her. The only reaction she cared about was Trent's, and his eyes hadn't left her.

Like a Judas, she'd betrayed him. And she didn't even have thirty pieces of silver to show for her treachery. She'd spoken out against the man she loved and for what—a town?

Yet she felt a glow of satisfaction. And as others stood and supported her position, Carla knew she had voiced the feelings of the majority.

The vote of the board actually took very little time once the discussion ended. "Zoning variance for Baker Labs denied," read the chairman. "Meeting dismissed." His gavel sounded one last time and cheers and applause took over.

"You're right," Bob Dolman said, after pushing his way to her side. "What we need in Roseville are small businesses, not large. And we're going to get them, thanks to Campbell."

"I don't understand," said Carla, trying to see which way Trent went after he left his chair.

"Because of all the publicity generated by the possibility of having a chemical plant here, people now know where Roseville is. Why, in the last week alone I've received over a dozen inquiries from small businesses; merchants who wanted to know more about our town. Sure, some of them won't come now that Baker Labs won't be coming—but others will. We're forming a committee. Felix Gordon and I decided that, right after your speech. We'll publicize Roseville, let others know what an ideal location this is, what a wonderful community. We're going to grow, Carla, just you watch. Two years from now Roseville will be a different place."

Without the presence of Trent Campbell. Carla wished she could share Bob's enthusiasm, but her own loss was too great. Desperately she looked around for Trent, needing to talk to him...to explain her reasons for speaking out against Baker Labs. As she moved away from Bob, others stopped to shake her hand and talk to her, but her responses were mechanical, her attention focused on finding Trent.

"Miss Parker, how do you think this will affect your relationship with Mr. Campbell?" one television reporter shouted, stopping her progress and pushing a microphone her way.

"Is it true you and Mr. Campbell are lovers?" asked a newspaper reporter, pressing forward.

A camera flashed and Carla backed up, blinking her eyes. "Please...I just want—"

"Miss Parker, when did you first decide to oppose Baker Labs?"

Turning, Carla pushed her way through the crowd, away from the reporters. Everybody, it seemed, was pressing in on her, cornering her. Suddenly she felt an overwhelming need to escape and rushed toward an open door.

Outside the building she stopped, her breathing ragged. Slowly she regained her composure as she glanced around the parking lot. Cars were leaving, their headlights cutting through the darkness. She knew she couldn't go back inside, not now. She would have to see Trent later. Turning her back on the school buildings, Carla walked toward her house.

When she started down her street, the sounds and lights of the traffic were left behind. A dog barked, crickets sang and the cool night breeze fanned her face. She sighed and slowed her steps. *Quiet rural Roseville, Indiana.* What a ruckus her little speech had raised. Tonight's meeting would be the center of conversation for weeks to come. Looking around her at the neatly kept houses, Carla wondered why she'd felt the need to defend this way of life.

Without thinking, she reached up and removed the pins from her hair, letting it fall softly to her shoulders. She hadn't meant to oppose Trent, but in a way he was to blame for her behavior. Three weeks ago Carla Parker would have thought only of her career, the heck with a town.

Carla bit her lower lip and gazed up at the moon. It was nearly full—a lovers' moon. *Damn Trent.* He'd shown her that a man could cook and sew and still be strong and that she could express her feelings and not be weak.

Well, she'd certainly been emotional tonight, praising small-town friendliness and lauding the virtues of rural life. She...a city girl. No...*woman*, she corrected herself, then smiled. That was Trent's way—supporting her "liberated woman" views, yet making her laugh at them. She'd laughed a lot since meeting Trent. It was his smile she would miss the most, that sexy, half-curve of his lips.

But Trent wouldn't be smiling tonight. No more than Thorton Wood would be, once he heard what she'd said at the meeting. She sighed as she walked up her steps. Car lights turned down the street and she hurried to let herself into the house.

It was hard to say what would happen to her job. If new companies came to Roseville—and they certainly should—Wood wouldn't have to close the branch. But she had spoken against Baker Labs, and that had certainly been against her boss's wishes. In the morning she would have to call him—explain her reasons.

She'd barely turned on the hall light when the telephone rang. Half hoping it was Trent, half dreading the possibility, Carla answered it.

"Miss Parker?" asked an unfamiliar voice. "This is Phil Goodman of the *Gazette*. I'd like to ask you a few questions."

"No...please," she groaned, putting her hand to her head. "No questions...not tonight."

"But, Miss Parker, you owe us an explanation. Tonight you swayed the vote against your fiancé's company. I'd like to know why."

"We are not engaged," Carla cried, then slammed down the receiver.r

Never have been...never will be. A headache was forming, her temples throbbing. She took two aspirins and the phone rang again.

"Yes?"

"Perhaps if I came over we could talk," answered the voice of the reporter.

"No!" Again she hung up, then, as an afterthought, pulled the phone jack from the wall. What she needed now was time to think. Closing her eyes, she leaned back against the counter. *No. I don't want to think, I want to forget.*

Forget all the hours of happiness, the feeling of belonging. He'd never said he loved her; yet she knew he felt the same way she did. He had to.

The doorbell jarred her thoughts. Snapping open her eyes, Carla started toward the hallway, then hesitated. It could be the reporter. Cautiously she called through the door, "Who's there?"

"Me, and if you don't open this door immediately, everyone in the neighborhood is going to know," snapped Trent.

Without question, Carla let him in.

"What happened?" he demanded. "I saw you bolt out of the gym, then you were gone."

"The reporters, their questions...I just couldn't take it," she confessed. "Oh, Trent, I'm sorry. I wasn't going to say anything tonight. I didn't want to speak out against you. If only Miss Atherby hadn't—"

Carla's voice cracked and the tears that had been so near the edge were released. Trent put his arms around her, gathering her close. "Hey, don't cry," he murmured, kissing the salty drops that slid down her cheeks. "You said what you believed, and obviously a lot of other people felt the same way or they wouldn't have agreed with you."

"But if I hadn't—" she choked.

"Someone else probably would have." He rocked her in his arms, kissing her face, her neck and her ears.

Stunned by his lack of anger, Carla clung to him, her tears slowly subsiding. And when he offered her his handkerchief, she took it, blew her nose and dried her eyes. Finally she looked at him. "You're not mad at me?"

"Only for running off." He grinned mischievously. "Or were you racing home to fix me a late night snack, get my slippers and turn down the bed?"

"Trent, I don't understand. Why aren't you more upset?"

"Because I agree with you," he calmly stated.

"You agree?" Wide-eyed, Carla stared at him.

He took her hand and together they went into the living room. There he removed his coat and tie and loosened the top buttons of his shirt. Carla glanced through the window at the lights in Miss Atherby's house and, as Trent made himself comfortable on the couch, she closed her drapes.

"But if you agree with me why did you go through with the meeting tonight?" she asked, still confused by his philosophical acceptance of what had happened.

"Because it wasn't up to you or me if Baker Labs should come to Roseville. It was up to the people who live here. Come over here and sit down." He patted the cushion beside him. "After being trounced by the multitudes, I need some loving."

Carla did as he said, kicking off her heels as she snuggled up next to him. His arm rested around her shoulders, keeping her close, and he kissed her once, before going on. "I knew how you felt. Last night, whether you realize it or not, you were practicing your speech. What I didn't know was if you could be honest about your feelings or if your career was more important."

"My career has suffered a definite setback," she mused, thinking of Wood and his certain reaction to the vetoed rezoning.

Trent chuckled. "So has Baker Labs, although I warned them last weekend that I didn't think the deal would go through."

"What will you do now?" The thought of Trent leaving Roseville made Carla's uncertain future even more bleak.

"As you suggested. I'll contact a national real estate agency and have their salespeople look for a large parcel of land on the outskirts of a city. We'll find something."

"In a way it's the Claytons who lose," Carla felt sorry for them. Henry and Mary had been looking forward to moving south, where the winters were warmer.

"Perhaps not. I called a friend of mine and told him about the Clayton farm. He flew into Fort Wayne this morning and I spent the day showing him around. For years Jim has talked about leaving the stock market and becoming a gentleman farmer. I think the Clayton farm is just what he's been looking for. At least he liked what he saw today. Saturday he's bringing his wife to look over the house. Would you be willing to act as hostess and help me entertain them while they're in town?"

"You'll still be in Roseville?" She d expected him to leave immediately. His reason for being in Roseville had ended tonight; there was no need for more soil samples or environmental studies.

"Of course I'll be here. I still have some unfinished business to tend to—banking business." He grinned, a teasing glint in his eyes. "Do you know any way to lure a determined feminist bank manager away from Roseville, Indiana? Once I suggested carrying her off, but she flatly rejected that idea. I might attempt bribery. I know the president of a very large bank and trust in Philadelphia and I'm sure he would hire her in a minute. But I'm afraid she'll tell me to go jump in a lake. What I would like—"

He paused and she lifted an eyebrow. "Yes?"

"What I would like," he continued, his voice more than a little husky, "is to marry you and take you back to Philadelphia as my wife."

She took in the words, not really believing them. But the expression on his face told her he wasn't joking, that he meant what he'd said. "We've only known each other a little more than three weeks," she murmured, her heart lodged in her throat.

"Three weeks—three years. It wouldn't matter. I think I started falling in love with you the moment I walked into your office and you pushed those over-sized glasses of yours back on your nose and announced you were C.J. Parker."

His hand strayed over her face, his fingertips lightly caressing her cheeks. "I don't want you to give up your career. You've got the drive and potential to make it to the top. What I want is to share the future with you. I love you, Carla."

She started to speak, but he went on.

"Maybe you don't love me, but what we have is special, and in time—"

"I do love you," she whispered.

"You what?" He stared at her, not certain he'd heard correctly.

"I love you." Carla said it louder, the happiness she felt showing on her face. "And I accept your proposal. I accept... I accept... I accept!"

Immediately the tension melted from his body and he held her close, kissing her and murmuring endearments. And when he paused, Carla asked, "You're serious about my working... about my career?"

"Very." He kissed her forehead, then tilted her face back, so that he could study her expression. "I know you wouldn't be content to stay at home. As soon as I find a new location for Baker Labs, I'll be leaving the field and taking over dad's job. He's made it clear he wants to retire this year. I would like children, Carla."

He watched her closely, fearing she would refuse his request, but Carla only smiled. "Bankers are very good at making little investments grow."

With a sigh of relief, Trent chuckled, then kissed her again, his mouth hungry and possessive this time. Immediately she felt an overpowering need to be a part of him. Her nipples grew taut beneath the cotton of her dress and pressed against the lace of her bra. Warm, fiery sensations snaked up between her legs, exciting her.

"You don't know how many times this last week I've nearly asked you to marry me," he hoarsely whispered. "But I was afraid you would choose to stay here, where you knew you had a future. In a way I was glad when they voted against Baker Labs."

"I would have said yes, even if things had turned out differently, even if the zoning had been approved." She groaned as he kissed the hollow of her throat.

Trent released the buttons of her dress. "Have you ever made love in the living room?"

"Trent!" She gasped as he slipped her dress off her shoulders. "Here? On the couch?"

"Or the rug." He smiled. "I'm spending the night, too."

"Already giving orders?" But she wasn't really upset. "What will the neighbors say?"

"That it was such a shame." He mimicked Miss Atherby's mannerisms and speech. "Carla was such a lovely young woman. So prim and proper, until that stranger came to town. Lord knows what went on in that house, but one day he left town and she ran off with him. They got married, I hear. Had to, I'm sure."

They both laughed. Trent was right. No matter what she did or didn't do tonight, after she left Roseville, tongues would wag for months to come. This time Carla didn't care what others said or thought. She'd found a man who could accept her as she was, who loved her and wanted to share, not dominate, her life.

Clothes were dropped helter-skelter on the floor. The longing growing in both of them demanded satisfaction. Trent crushed her to the couch with his weight, but Carla willingly held him to her, spreading her hands across the width of his shoulders, digging her fingers into his taut muscles. She tasted him, her tongue caressing his neck, and drew in a deep breath, holding it for a moment to enjoy the scent of him. He was man and she was woman.

His own lips nibbled delicately up the graceful line of her throat, pulling on a tiny earring, until the silver bauble dropped from her lobe and onto the floor. Carla sighed in pleasure and he arched himself over her, gazing down, his eyes hungrily taking in the beauty of her feminine proportions.

Creamy white mounds rose and fell in tempo with her shallow breathing, their rosy red peaks enticing him to investigate closer. But his touch was not limited to one general area. Every inch of her body was explored, words of love mixed with plundering caresses.

Her legs parted invitingly, like a blossom enticing a bee, and he came to her, kissing, caressing, until she groaned out his name, begging for total satisfaction. And he brought it with a slow, driving pressure that fit masculine hard to feminine soft. Then he moved forcefully, masterfully within her and Carla curved her legs around his hips.

Her entire being was focused on one central point. Time became meaningless. Currents of excitement coursed through her body, promising, fulfilling. Then, at last, Trent cried out her name, his body rigid, and they both lost control. A violent convulsion turned to smaller spasms, then shivers. Every nerve ending tingled as she gasped for a breath. He loved her and she loved him. It was enough.

In weeks to come they would have a church wedding, resplendent with flowers and her mother's tears. Her sister would be the matron-of-honor and her father would give her away—a traditional gesture, not symbolic. She was no one's property, to be given or received—no man's chattel. In the business world she would have to prove she was equal or better than her male counterparts, but with Trent she could simply be a woman.

Harlequin Stationery Offer

Personalized Rainbow Memo Pads for you or a friend

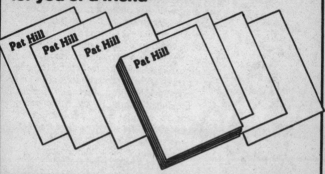

Picture your name in bold type at the top of these attractive rainbow memo pads. Each 4¼" x 5½" pad contains 150 rainbow sheets—yellow, pink, gold, blue, buff and white—enough to last you through months of memos. Handy to have at home or office.

Just clip out three proofs of purchase (coupon below) from an August or September release of Harlequin Romance, Harlequin Presents, Harlequin Superromance, Harlequin American Romance, Harlequin Temptation or Harlequin Intrigue and add $4.95 (includes shipping and handling), and we'll send you *two* of these attractive memo pads imprinted with your name.